STORM CLOUDS GATHER

JENNIFER ASHCROFT

Chapters

Chapter 24 Fixing Roots

Prologue

What're the chances of a peaceful and fulfilling life now. Is it even possible to be happy ever again? You've lost so much and you find yourself living alone in an area which means just about nothing to you. You don't even know how to start rebuilding. You're nothing more than a child, unschooled in the sensible moves in life. You only have your own damaged personality which defines you and causes you to act accordingly. You're not really starting from zero because all of your history follows you around. You behave in certain ways and make decisions based upon past experiences. How can you escape your own personality, which is formed out of genetic factors and combined with the fears of your own unfortunate history. Can you run away from yourself?

This is a true story, some of the names have been changed.

Chapter 1

Easy Target

It was the summer of 1988 and I was almost twenty-four-years-old. A Worcester girl, living alone in an east-end council flat. And like thousands of others, in London, I worked Monday to Friday in my monotonous office job. I went to work to pay my bills. While weekends were spent doing the essentials in preparation for work on Monday mornings.

My flat was basic but, over time, I'd afforded myself cheap carpets and curtains and some essential furniture. It was certainly better than living in the derelict houses of the past. As long as I worked, I could pay my rent and that meant that those traumatic years of homelessness were hopefully now behind me. But the damage was done and I felt resigned to a lifetime of repetitive nightmares, indecisiveness, and ill-judged decisions.

I lived on the ground-floor, which didn't help with my feelings of vulnerability. I was paranoid about someone getting in through one of the easily accessible single-glazed windows. I suppose I would have felt a little safer being upstairs. There was only one flat above me, where a girl called Mandy lived. That wasn't her official name, it was an English version of her real name. She was of mixed-race heritage, although she was born and bred in east London with a strong cockney accent. She had a big family who all lived nearby and she had lots of old school-friends in the area too. She was the same age as myself and she had an infant boy-child, who was the age my two lost ones would have been by now. Her son was now a cute toddler. His baby-grows and baby clothes hanged out on our shared washing line in the back garden. The back garden was filled with stinging-nettles except for the broken-up concrete path which allowed us to walk to the line.

When I'd first lived at the flat, with my boyfriend Mark, I'd initially got on very well with Mandy. She'd known all about our sick twins and she'd been quite supportive. She would sometimes come into my place for a coffee and likewise I'd go upstairs for coffee with her. She'd been the one who'd called the police on several occasions when she'd heard my screams, during those domestic abuse months.

I don't know exactly why Mandy turned against me. But I noticed a change in her, soon after I finally broke up with Mark. Maybe she saw me as a threat now, she did have a boyfriend. My mother always said she'd lost several friends after Dad had left her, due to them now seeing her as a 'single-female threat.' We're animals at the end of the day. Or perhaps, Mandy's change in behaviour towards me, was something to do with her hearing me screaming while being beaten and seeing me in tears so often. She knew too much about me, she knew I had no one to defend me, emotionally or physically.

In my naivety I'd been natural, I'd been open and honest and I'd shown my vulnerabilities like a child does. I was an adult but I'd made no attempt to protect myself, I didn't have that protective nature, I just hadn't been taught it or learned it yet. I was like a tortoise muddling through life without its shell or any friends or family. Wondering why I kept getting hurt and feeling so much pain.

The bullied get bullied. The runt of the litter is an easy target and animals will even attack and kill a weak one. There's something in all of us which sometimes causes a dislike of the vulnerable. We have instincts which we don't fully understand and we Are animals at the end of the day.

Anyway, by now, Mandy was adding to my life's miseries. She was hounding me with her unfair behaviour and there was nothing much I could do about it. She'd have her family and friends over, even late on a Sunday night, when I'd have work the next day. Her music would blare out loud and continue after midnight. But when I played music, even during the day, she'd bang on my door and insist I turn it off. Saying her son was trying to sleep. In the end she'd just bang on her floor if I made any living sound at all.

Then Mandy threw an old three-piece-suite out and placed the old furniture in front of my living-room window where there was a small, shared concrete area. On warmer days she'd sit there laughing and joking with her friends, with music blaring. I'd close my windows and curtains for privacy and cover my ears but they still sounded like they were inside my flat. She obviously had something against me and I started to really hate her which isn't good for the soul is it.

Then Mandy got herself a little puppy dog which she often left home alone all day, whilst out visiting her family and friends, I assume. It would bark and howl for hours but she had no pity for the creature. That's where I drew the line. I knew that having dogs was against the council flat rules and so I called the council from my newly installed home-telephone. I made a complaint or you could say, I grassed-her-up for everything.

The council woman wrote everything down. She could hear the dog yapping in the background. 'Oh, I don't know how you can stand it?' She spoke. Not that there was anything much I could do about it - this complaint was my one and only option of a cause of action. Then she took note of our ethnic statuses (as that had started to become a thing of late) to move forward with my complaint. Apparently, there was a checklist to be ticked off during the conversation. As I was 'white English' and Mandy was of an 'ethnic' background the lady said that she couldn't tick any box for 'racism' so she ticked the 'sexism' box. This didn't make much sense to me, seeing as Mandy and I were both female. But it didn't have to make sense. The woman said, she knew what she was doing and she'd be writing a strong letter to Mandy. She also said that she would protect me by not giving any details of who'd complained. The whole telephone conversation, the tick boxes etcetera, would all be kept confidential.

That's when the trouble really started. I received a copy of the ill written, confidential letter to Mandy on the same day that she received hers. The dog was mentioned, along with some ridiculous allegations of sexism. My name wasn't mentioned but Mandy would have to have been a fool not to have known it was me who'd made an official complaint against her. Mandy was a lot of things but she was no fool. She was on my doorstep within an hour of the postman's delivery. 'I know it was you who grassed-me-up to the council, you better watch ya back!' Mandy was holding the letter and threatening me with all sorts, while her boyfriend stood on her outdoor steps, ready to back her up if necessary. She really was a vile bully. I was afraid to complain again after that. Mandy had a big family behind her and I had no one. The poor puppy increased in size and continued barking and howling even louder. I made no further attempt to deal with the situation and I heard no more from the council, on the subject.

I Just kept going. Work, supermarket and back to the flat. I was invariably unhappy but somehow still hopeful that something miraculous would happen. I knew what I needed to solve my problems in my life. I needed a loving family to love and protect me and keep me company. The only way to create that scenario was through finding Mr Right, having his children and being adopted into his family. This learned, single-minded desperation would almost be the death of me.

Chapter 2

Loneliness

Many animals, especially mammals, must live in groups for their own mental and physical well-being. Sheep are herd animals. If you separate one sheep from its flock, it will not live a happy life and it will likely die within a short space of time. It's so cruel to keep a sheep outside of its flock that famers (who're unable to integrate it for whatever reason) will have it slaughtered out of kindness.

Humans are pack-animals and very few of us are cut-out for a completely solo life. But I suppose there's a big difference between those who choose a life of solitude and those who feel forced into it.

Loneliness is such a terribly sad affair; it eats away at you from the inside out. It can cause all kinds of ailments from depression to autoimmune diseases and even to heart disease and cancers. I already had my first autoimmune disease, I'd noticed that when my skin came into contact with anything cold, it quickly went red and itchy, and left unchecked, I'd get hives. I'd first noticed it in the months and years following my mother's death. She died when I was fifteen and after that

I'd moved in between relatives, who clearly didn't want me or weren't in a position to be able to accommodate me. Then Foster care and again backwards and forwards in between my sister and father, with the feeling of being a burden on everyone. I'd been deliberately locked outside of my father's house one snowy night. It was my first sad winter without my mum. I was so confused and distressed and my skin began to itch. That was the first time that I'd noticed this new ailment but I'd had more pressing issues to concern myself with at that time, so it got left on the back-burner.

By seventeen I'd come to the realisation that, other than my dead mum, no one loved me. I'd suffered terribly from grief, worry and misery. So, with hindsight, I see a connection between stress-hormones and autoimmune diseases but also nutrition (or lack of) probably plays its part. I hadn't taken care of myself; I hadn't concerned myself with vitamin intake at all. I just ignored this strange reaction/ailment for several years until something happened which forced me to seek medical attention.

I'd been a strong swimmer, since childhood, and a big fan of swimming pools. During my terrible teenage years, the permanence of Worcester Swimming Baths was the only place that felt like home. The strong smell of the chlorine/ bleach comforted me in some strange way. And the lifeguards new me there and always seemed pleased to see me at a time when I'd felt unwelcome everywhere else.

Anyway, more recently, I'd gone to an out-door open-air swimming pool in east London, and although it was almost summer, the water was really cold. I'd dived in and halfway up the length of the pool I'd felt my skin prickling. I made a conscious decision to finish off the length before getting out and I forced myself to continue swimming. It didn't seem worth paying to go in, if I didn't at least finish off one length.

At the deep end, I climbed the metal steps and then started my way urgently back to my towel. My skin was already a blotchy-red colour and the hives were coming up. But worse than that, my throat was closing up and I was beginning to feel faint. I was aware of people looking at my body redness. I felt a bit panicky due to my throat tightening. Of course, I knew no-one there and didn't expect anyone to quickly come to my recue. But I managed to get to my towel and I quickly wrapped myself up. I was shaking all over but I dried my feet and hurriedly put on my socks. Then I just rocked myself back and forth and rubbed my itchy spots with my towel, uncontrollably. Eventually I warmed up a little, got dressed and the redness eased then disappeared.

That day had led me to the doctor's surgery. He'd told me that my condition was called 'Cold Urticaria,' he'd put me on antihistamines for the winter months and offered me an EpiPen for emergencies such as that one. I was to be really careful, in future, with unexpected and especially all-over body attacks. If you think about it, it kind of makes sense that I'd developed a reaction to the cold. Because I'd felt so cold, both physically and mentally, (unloved) since my early teenagerhood. The ailment was like a psychosomatic illness but it was very real, dangerously so.

But it's only with hindsight that I see the connection between emotional and physical health. Anyway, even if I'd seen the connection back in my teens, there was nothing I could have done to ease my stress levels. I often thought back on what I should have done differently, after my mum died, when I was fifteen and the years after that. But I was still officially a child and at the mercy of adults. My brain never rested when I thought of all the traumas. I tried to solve the puzzle on decisions I should have made and where I should have lived. But I only came up with the - not knowing. And 'not knowing' really didn't help me with putting it all to rest. I couldn't stop reliving it all. And without roots and guidance I would continue to make decisions led by emotion. Often wrong decisions, usually involving the male of the species.

I now had my own council flat, in the heart of east London, where I lived alone. I was by nature a people-person or maybe I'd become a people-pleaser as a kind of survival mechanism. I'd known I needed help and assistance to survive since I'd been left, in effect, orphaned. I'd been left moving from home to home from the age of fifteen onwards. I suppose that I'd learned that being 'agreeable' was more likely to keep a roof over my head. But my charm, coupled with my depression, had been a confusing combination for those allowing me 'temporarily' into their homes. Nevertheless, I remained the agreeable personality type and as such I was driven to be in a pack or at least to be in a couple. I certainly wasn't the loner type.

Ideally, I wanted a big happy family. Which was going to be a tall-order, considering I'd completely lost my immediate family i.e., mother, father and sister, I'd lost my extended family too, uncles, aunties and cousins, they were all out. And I'd lost my own babies and their father.

I used to watch repeats of a television series called 'The Little House on the Prairie' because my dream was to have a perfect family like they had in that series. I never really dreamed about being rich. My dream was simple - a family, my family. A priceless situation which cannot be bought and from the starting point I was in, it could never happen. I should have given up back then but I still dreamed and believed it could still be possible. While my peers were dreaming of holidays, diamond rings and fast cars, I wanted to join the Amish. But one has to be born into the Amish and no one can 'join them' for obvious reasons. Their whole society would soon fall apart if they allowed damaged heathens like me to come and infiltrate them.

There's no appropriate age to be lonely. But we tend to think of it as an older person's affliction. I was approaching my twenty-fourth birthday and had nothing planned. My loneliness coupled with my young abundance of hormones, dictated my next moves. I was driven to find a partner, a husband, I had to succeed in my desire and my need for my 'Little house on the prairie' type situation. But to be honest and with the benefit of hindsight, without parents, family or community, that possibility was gone - dead, already, unachievable, a farfetched notion.

Remember that fantasy I'd had as a child? I'd imagined ahead to my glorious wedding day. I was wearing a beautiful white dress made of satin and lace. I was being led up the aisle of Worcester cathedral, on the arm or my father. My mother and sister were wiping away their tears of joy in the front row of the ancient building. Friends and relatives had packed out every pew. That could never happen now, none of it. Mum was gone and I was estranged from my father and sister. And, from my move from Worcester (in the West Midlands) to London, I'd lost touch with every childhood friend I'd ever known.

Monday to Friday I was busy with my office job but

on weekends, besides food-shopping, there was nothing much to go out for. I was lonely as lonely could be and only spent my weekends preparing for work on Mondays.

So, I tried to make a social life for myself outside of work. I was still young and living in London, after all, and this should have been the best years of my life but I needed family, friends, people. I had a couple of female colleagues, of a similar age to myself, in my work office. So, I approached them but they seemed busy with their families and boyfriends. And neither of them even lived in my area, they both commuted into work from Essex every day. I didn't want to push too hard; I didn't want them thinking I was desperate. In just about every situation from job interviews to relationships, the more desperate you appear the less likely you are to succeed in your desired outcome.

I was young and free. I was living in London where the possibilities for entertainment were supposed to be endless. In central London - theatres, nightclubs and restaurants were in abundance. Even locally to me, there were plenty of lively pubs and clubs. But I didn't want to walk into a local pub by myself as young women didn't really do that, especially in those days. Apparently, people looked down on women who frequented pubs alone and I just couldn't face their negative assumptions.

There was a feeling of sadness inside me, a

pointlessness. When I look back on myself, I realise how depressed and vulnerable I was and how dangerous my circumstances were. I was young, attractive, alone, bereft, lonely, unloved, unwatched, uncared-for, vulnerable, sexually-active and emotionally weak. I'd been stripped of belongings, love, hope, dreams and self-respect. The roots of my faults were all due to the faults in my roots or lack of roots. Every decision I took, was taken through loneliness and with withered and unnourished roots. And any acquaintance, psychologist or counsellor who ever advised me, could never comprehend the gravity of my circumstances.

Chapter 3

Queen's Head

When my mum had been lonely and sad, after her divorce, she'd gone to pubs and clubs to look for a new man. So, I guess I learned (back in my tweens) that those were the places to go to solve my problem. I also learned, without realising it, that a woman must have a man or she will die. I'd learned that, by seeing how my mother fell apart when my father left us. I'd watched her desperately searching for the new, right man and failing. I'd watched her collapse from misery and depression and die with a broken-heart.

After several weekends of sitting indoors, by myself, I celebrated my twenty-fourth birthday alone in the flat. The next day was the last day in September and a Friday. I finally dug deep for some confidence and decided to go to one of the pubs I'd been in once or twice before, back in Stratford. The pub was called the Queen's Head and was near to the King Edward, known as the Eddie - my old haunt. It was a five-minute walk to the bus-stop and then a five-minute bus ride to get to the Queen's Head. Or the other alternative was a cut-through twenty-five-minute walk (or twenty minutes at a fast pace) but I decided on the bus option.

I felt awkward walking into the pub alone, as the mostly male heads turned to look at me. I pretended, to myself, that I was meeting a girlfriend and that friend would, of course, never show up. Something unfortunate must have happened to prevent her from showing. I started to believe this story myself.

As I walked into the pub, everyone instinctively turned to see who'd come through the door. I scanned the joint then lowered my eyes with awkwardness and embarrassment. Then almost immediately, I forced myself to hold my head up as if I had a genuine purpose being there. I was meeting my friend! I clocked the serving area and then noticed two guys sitting up at the bar on the high stools. One looked in his forties and his friend, mid-twenties. My hands were shaking as I stood near to them and ordered myself a Bacardi and Coke. By now I wouldn't have considered myself a drinker at all but this occasion definitely warranted a drop of alcohol.

'Hello, what's a nice-looking bird, like you, doing in ere all by er-self?' Said the younger of the two.

'Oh, I'm meeting my girl-friend here, she'll be along soon.' I said, as I stuck to my story.

As I got my purse out to pay for my drink, the younger guy told the barmaid to put it on his tab and I said 'Oh thanks.' He then got off of his bar-stool and politely offered for me to sit on it while I waited for my 'girl-friend' to arrive. I accepted the stool while he stood next to me and introduced himself and his older friend.

His name was Andy, born and bred in East London. He was average in height and well dressed in Levi jeans and a blue Ben Sherman tea-shirt. Yet he was ever so slightly chubby with dark-blond hair and a kindly smile. He said he had his own French-polishing business with his brother. He had his own flat which was within walking distance of the pub. His Scottish friend's name obviously wasn't Scott but that's what people called him and he seemed resigned to accepting it.

As the evening went on, all of my drinks went onto Andy's tab and of course my 'girl-friend' never showed up. At the end of the evening, I said I needed to get my bus home but Andy insisted that if I stayed for the lock-in, he would pay for my cab home later. I was enjoying his company and was just happy to be out of the flat so, of course, I stayed. The pub officially closed at eleven pm and just a few of us remained for the lock-in/'private party.'

Andy was funny, (probably more so because he was obviously drunk) kind and extremely generous with his money. He wasn't bad looking either, he certainly had an endearing charm about him. He dressed himself well and smelt of lovely expensive aftershave. He obviously looked after himself with decent clothes, a close shave and a sharp haircut.

I never spent a penny that night. It was a Friday and we lived in a 'pub culture' where most young people got drunk on weekends. So, it wasn't unusual to see someone that drunk and considering the amount he'd drank; he was doing well. He was still in control of his faculties, still fully compos mentis. Little did I know that he was drinking like this most nights of the week.

Although I considered myself a non-drinker, by the end of the lock-in, I was plastered. Andy and his Scottish friend had been propping up the bar since before I'd arrived that night. On my arrival, Andy had been drinking pints but by the time of the lock-in, he'd moved onto Vodka-shots. I suppose there's only so much liquid a body can hold.

At the end of the lock-in, Andy ordered and paid for my taxi-cab home, on the promise that I'd meet him again the following evening - Saturday.

On my arrival at the Queen's Head, the following evening, Andy and Scott were sitting in the exact same position as the night before. Andy's face lit up as I walked in and they both looked pleased to see me. Andy immediately ordered me a Bacardi and coke. But I had a terrible hang-over from the previous evening and said I'd prefer just a Coke. Andy said another alcoholic drink was the best thing to cure a hang-over, so I accepted the Bacardi and I have to say it did help to remove my headache.

After a few more drinks, Andy said he'd like to take me out for a meal. So, we went to the Indian restaurant next door. I was no expert on Indian food and didn't want to risk trying the strange sounding meal-items on the menu. So, I ordered from their English selection, chicken and chips. Andy had obviously eaten there several times before as the waiters recognised him and he knew his way around the menu. He ordered something called a Tika Masala and lots of side dishes with unusual names, which seemed very exotic to me at the time.

As we left the restaurant, we popped into an off-licence where Andy bought a huge bottle of Vodka and a large bottle of lemonade. We took a taxi to my flat and spent the night drinking together and chatting.

On the Sunday, Andy suggested we go to the pub for Sunday lunch and that evening he stayed over again and we were now officially a 'couple.' It was great to have some company, it gave the flat a completely different, warm, atmosphere.

Andy's brother picked Andy up from my flat and they went off to work together on the Monday morning. And I went off to my office job. Andy and I had an agreement to meet up again on that coming Friday night. I was looking forward to it. I felt enthusiastic to think that I had someone now, I had a spring in my step and couldn't wait to see him again. As I arrived home that day, my recently installed home-telephone was already ringing and it was Andy.

'Me bird's chucked me out Jen,' Andy blurted out.

'Your bird! - I didn't know you had a girlfriend!' I was thrown into a quandary.

'Yeah, she's chucked me out cause I stayed out wiv you over the weekend and now I've got nowhere ta go' He continued.

I fell silent for a few seconds, while I pondered and tried to process what Andy was saying. He'd previously mentioned that he had a flat, near the Queen's Head but I'd assumed that he'd lived there alone. Now it seemed it was his girlfriend's flat! I tried to think what my response should be. I had the feeling that his girlfriend hadn't known about me at all, why would she? Why would he tell her? He could easily have said that he'd spent the night with Scott or on another friend's settce.

I had the feeling that Andy was just keen to be with me rather than his girlfriend. I think he wanted to jump-ship and as I had my own flat and I was keen on him, he guessed I might easily be persuaded. He knew it. It was like offering candy to a baby. But in some way, was I being duped? I guess I should have responded like this - 'You've deceived me, it's your problem.' Maybe I should have put the telephone down and never seen him again!

But I liked Andy so much and he obviously liked me if he was willing to take so many risks. He'd been treating me well and I was already attached to him. Anyhow, I felt somehow responsible for his sudden homelessness. And I didn't want to go back to living the solitary life!

'Ok well you better come here and we'll talk about it' I said.

Within half an hour, Andy arrived in a taxi, along with several bags and we talked. 'Maybe you should go and stay with your brother for the time being?' I suggested.

'Nah he lives wiv is Mrs and she's pregnant and about to drop.'

'Oh well, I guess you can stay here, with me, for now?' I suggested.

We were now living together.

Chapter 4

What Luxury

My flat was basic. I had the essentials but my furniture was mostly second-hand. My curtains were simple and my wall-to-wall carpets were of the cheapest cord variety. But I did appreciate what I had and I felt some achievement in buying and paying for it all, from my own hard work.

But within a few months, Andy would turn the council flat into a luxurious apartment! He decorated and replaced the cheap flooring with most expensive shagpile carpets. My cheap curtains went into the dustbin and were swapped with classy replacements. Bit by bit he'd bring home quality pieces of French polished furniture, which were 'extras from work' and as a new piece came in, my cheaper versions of the same stuff, would go to the tip. I particularly liked the new French polished telephone table which I positioned in the corridor, just inside the front door. My telephone apparatus went on top with a notepad and pen. I was pleased to see the back of the second-hand three-piece suite as the dark green, leather Chesterfield arrived. The flat looked great and the situation with the upstairs neighbours completely calmed down too.

Everyone seemed to drink at that age and in those days. On first meeting a new person, it was usual to ask 'Where do you drink?' It was just a normal part of British drinking culture. But I suppose I knew, when I first met Andy, that he drank a bit more than what was within the normal and acceptable range.

I was now a strict vegetarian and didn't allow meat inside the flat (something I'd eventually taken up because of my previous vegetarian boyfriend.) I was no longer a smoker and I wasn't bothered about alcohol - I could take it or leave it. All three of these non-activities (not drinking, not smoking and not eating meat) seemed to bother Andy, especially when he'd had a drink. He saw me as a goody-goody. He obviously didn't know me so well. He didn't understand that I avoided drugs, cigarettes and alcohol just to avoid panic attacks and to try and have some control over my nerves. Although I tried to explain, he just didn't get it. If you've never suffered a panic-attack or these kind of mental health issues, I guess it is difficult to comprehend.

Within days of knowing Andy, I'd realised that he regularly drank to excess and within a few weeks I understood that he had a serious drink-problem. But as he would upset me with his drunken behaviour, he'd follow it by coming home with some luxury item for the flat. This good action would override the bad and confuse my brain. Then I'd do my best to put his mean words behind me and hope for the best.

Andy's friend, Scott, was clearly an alcoholic and I saw him as the bad influence. I considered him to be the problem. So, I did my upmost to separate the two friends. I would try to prevent Andy from going out without me and I'd do my best to slow down his excessive drinking while I was out with him. Scott would usually turn up and really, they were both unstoppable. I ceased drinking completely, to show a good example but my sobriety only seemed to get Andy's back up, every time, when he became increasingly more intoxicated.

One day Andy came home a little later from work than usual, on a Wednesday evening. I always got in before him and I'd cooked one of the vegetarian concoctions I'd taught myself. The meal consisted of fried onions and fried mushrooms with an added tin of baked beans and some basic herbs and spices. With bread and butter on the side, I found it surprisingly tasty. But Andy wasn't impressed. He was clearly in a bad mood and it was all directed at me and my lack of catering skills.

'I come ome from work and you serve me wiv a pile a Shit on me plate!' He complained. Then, after repeating that sentence in several different formats, he threw the whole plate and food into the kitchen sink. I just felt nervous and gutted but I said nothing as my eyes filled up. 'I need meat!' he continued. 'I don't wanna come ome after an ard day's work, to a pile a Shit on me plate!'

'What a horrible thing to say,' I said, 'I'm sick of you.' Well, that seemed to hit a nerve and before I knew it, Andy had gone out. I guessed he'd get himself a kebab on his way to the Queen's head.

Firstly, I cleaned up the kitchen and then, after an hour or two, I made my way to the pub. When I arrived, Andy and Scott were already on shots, which meant that they were already full of beer. Scott got me a Bacardi and coke but I didn't want it with Bacardi. So Andy knocked it back in an aggressive way as if he were somehow teaching me a lesson or something. I ordered myself a coke and stuck to soft drinks until Andy agreed to call it a night.

Eventually we took a taxi home. But that's when the real trouble started. A row broke out between the two of us in the back seat of the taxi. When we got home it really kicked off and before I knew it, we were screaming and shouting at each other. Then suddenly we were in the bedroom and I was thrust into a laying down position on the bed. Andy was fuming and standing over me with his fist held against my face. The whites of his eyes were bloodshot-red and he was literally foaming at the mouth with anger. He was spitting as he shouted in temper and threatening like a bull, ready to attack.

Andy was furious because of the things I'd said during the initial argument. And especially because I'd said I was sick of him. I was angry with him too. I knew I was inept at cooking but I'd been doing my best. Andy also seemed angry that I didn't drink or smoke and because I was a vegetarian. He was saying bizarre things like, 'You're a hippy, you're a member of Green Peace you are' and 'You don't drink or smoke cause You're a Christian, you love Jesus' And, why don't ya fuck off back to Worcester! None of his words made much sense but still, like a fool, I continued retorting.

Andy had fully lost control and I knew that I was about to get battered. I suddenly realised, I should stop arguing back, I should stop verbally defending myself. I should stop reacting to the ridiculous and horrible things he was saying. I should stop reacting to the cues of aggression. I had to think fast to prevent being beaten. I'd been through this before with the previous boyfriend. I'd always argued back. At this point I would normally hit out or push or slap as defence but I'd learned the error in those moves.

Girls slap boys at their peril. Women slap men at their peril. Men are physically so much stronger than us females and we should always bear that in mind. Add their anger or alcohol to that and they can be easily agitated and violent towards you in an argument. When I'd slapped Mark, that had given him the green-light to hit me back, ten times harder. After that one green-light, I was continually at his mercy. I was sure Andy was capable of the same or even worse, so instead of goading him, I now just covered my head instinctively and cried out, 'I'm sorry, I'm sorry, I'm sorry, I'm sorry!' Andy continued standing over me with his spitting mouth and vile words. But my pathetic behaviour prevented the violence which I knew was close in his intention.

After I'd begged for mercy, the atmosphere calmed down and we soon went to bed. We weren't speaking to each other at this point and as soon as Andy's head hit the pillow he slept quickly and deeply. While I lay awake half of the night thinking of all the mean things he'd said and how his face had looked as he'd foamed at the mouth, in extreme anger, with his bloodshot red eyes. I now knew I was in danger. Out of loneliness I'd let a monster in.

As a fully functioning - suspected alcoholic, self-employed young man, Andy was up early next day, preparing himself for work. I pretended to be asleep and kept my face hidden under the quilt to hide my tears. His brother's car pulled up as usual and the two of them went off to their work studio.

As I heard the car pull away, I got up and ready for work. I did my best to hide my sadness all day in the office. But I never was very good at hiding my feelings and ended up wearing my heart on my sleeve as usual. My female colleagues showed care and interest in my predicament, especially my friend, Meena. But her Asian life had been so different to mine that I'm not sure she could really comprehend much of my situation at all.

Andy was home before me that day. He must have left work early or taken the afternoon off. I went in and saw him in my peripherals. He was sitting quietly in the living room but I didn't look at him directly. I didn't speak and neither did he. I was really angry and upset with him and the atmosphere, from my side, was icy.

Instead of attempting any conversation, I went straight to the bedroom with the intention of not communicating with Andy for the rest of the night, at least. But as I opened the bedroom door, I was shocked to see what I saw on the double bed. The biggest and most beautiful bouquet of fresh, multi-coloured, flowers I'd ever seen, with a card which read, 'To Jen, I'm so sorry, Love Andy X,' Lying next to the bouquet was the biggest box of chocolates I ever saw. Almost a metre square, a single layer of most expensive chocolates.

The chocolate box had a picture on the front of it, an idyllic country cottage with a thatched roof, surrounded by multi-coloured roses. A happy-looking couple stood at the wooden door with big smiles on their faces. While two content children (a boy and a girl) played in the flower filled garden at their feet. I closed my eyes and for a moment, I was the young women in the chocolate box picture. I was surrounded by stability, love, happiness, and roses.

I came out of my moments of fantasy and became overwhelmed with perplexing emotions. One of which was terrible guilt because I wasn't speaking to Andy and I'd been thinking bad and angry thoughts about him all day. Now I felt sympathy for him. He'd made such an effort to go out and buy these beautiful and thoughtful gifts and he must have spent a fortune on them. I started to feel sorry for him and angry with myself. I felt rising guilt. I've since discovered that abused females often suffer misplaced guilt but I didn't know that at the time so I trusted that I felt guilty because I'd somehow done something wrong.

The chocolates and the flowers were beautiful. But along with my feelings of guilt, I still knew that the way Andy had behaved last night was truly unacceptable. I knew that these gifts were 'sorry presents' and I knew that what had happened last night, would probably happen again. But I was exhausted from the previous night's arguing, I had a confusing array of emotions and I just wanted peace. I sat on the bed, in between the chocolates and the flowers, and I just quietly sobbed my heart out.

After a few minutes, Andy came in, he apologised and then he embraced me. Initially I held onto my depleting anger and self-protection, but within a matter of seconds my defences crumbled and I collapsed in his comforting arms. As he held onto me, he told me how sorry he was for his aggression and threatening behaviour. And he promised that it would never happen again. He became charming and enthusiastic. He said he was going to get rid of my second-hand television and buy us a new, top of the range set. But I explained that what I really wanted was for him to quit drinking and he insisted that he would definitely cut down. Then I felt some instant relief at the current crises being over but, in some way, I knew in my heart, that it was just the beginning.

The flowers smelled like sweet perfume for a couple of days. Then, as their roots had been cut, they started to give off that putrid fragrance which always takes me right back to funerals and graveyards. I much preferred the smell of flowers still being nourished through their life-source in the earth. Nourished flowers flourish like nourished people do. Those without roots really have no chance. Why do we cut the beautiful things, destroying their roots only for a selfish couple of days of beauty and pleasant fragrance? Followed by wilting and fetid lifeless and useless slimy roots struggling to direct attention to the top. Those happy and pretty flowers, cut in their prime, cannot be salvaged once their roots are gone. Just like me, they could not be replanted and nothing could save them. Without good, reliable roots everything's wrong! Nothing makes me heave like the stench of dying flowers, the smell of slow death.

Almost automatically, I started to feel less physically attracted to Andy. His face became less endearing to me and his expensive aftershave started to make me feel nauseous. How my physical interest in him had rapidly taken a nosedive soon became obvious to him. I tried to fake it and I hoped my desire would return but it seems once it's lost it's gone forever. He realised, almost immediately, that I was starting to refuse him and he dealt with his feelings of rejection very ill indeed.

'I need sex!' Andy shouted, one evening during another argument. I'd been repeatedly making up excuses for refusal and he was getting frustrated.

'Oh my God, what are you? A caveman!' I replied as I put my hand to my forehead.

He continued ranting and raving. His behaviour really wasn't helping his cause.

I tried to keep calm but I just felt so stressed and sad. I thought we should probably break up but I still had feelings for Andy. And he'd made the flat so luxurious and I felt guilty about that. And he planned on doing so much more in the flat and luxury holidays were on the agenda too. Also, my nasty neighbour was behaving herself, while he was around and I didn't want to go back to being at her mercy. I had to think fast about what I should do next.

I needed a long and deep chat with a reliable girlfriend. I was still in touch with my old friend Jaz, who I'd been good friends with when I'd lived back in the student house in Crystal Palace. More than four years ago now. Since she was no longer an art student, she now lived back at home, with her parents in Bristol.

Jaz and I used to dream about travelling when we'd lived together at the student house. Since then, she'd done some serious travelling around India by herself, while I had travelled nowhere except for in and around London. Oh, and one disastrous trip to France one time.

I started to call Jaz regularly form my work telephone. I'd tell her the ins and outs of my difficult situation with Andy. And she would listen intently and advise.

JENNIFER ASHCROFT

Chapter 5

Tropical

I'd always thought I would travel the world but then my life got in the way and I became increasingly neurotic. I'd actually recently paid for and received a visa/one year work-permit to go to Australia but I hadn't gone because of all of my fears and I couldn't face potential homelessness on my return. Without a safety net I was unable to risk walking the tightrope of life. I was unable to try so many things, which a young person should try. I wasn't in a position to be able to risk failure. Without the safety net of parents, if I fell, I would surely crash into the rocks. Whereas if I'd have had the net, I could have and would have soared the skies. If I'd have had parents to come home to, I think I would have travelled a lot. But then again, if I'd have had parents, I wouldn't be in the position I was now in, living in a dysfunctional relationship in the sad flat in misery town.

If I had gone off to Australia, the council would've probably taken the flat from me. I couldn't afford to pay the rent while away without subletting and subletting was strictly against the council's rules. I might have got away with it if I hadn't got a nasty neighbour upstairs who hated me so much. She was bound to grass me up the second she realised I was gone. One is not given council flats to sublet or leave unoccupied while other potential tenants are left homeless. So, a year was definitely impossible.

When I'd first met Andy, I'd told him of my dream of traveling to Australia and he'd suggested that I could go for a month instead of a year. That would count as a 'holiday' and the council wouldn't evict me for that even if they did find out. Andy had encouraged me to find the courage to go. He'd said that he would take care of the flat while I was away. But then a couple of weeks after this offer had been suggested, we'd had our first argument and he'd said I was 'Out of order' for thinking I could just 'fuck off' for a month. So, I never went on my dream trip to Australia and my one-year visa eventually expired.

I often called Jaz from my work telephone and one day we got chatting about going away on holiday together. She really thought a break from Andy would do me good, so I got to checking the local travel agent's window. There was a very reasonably priced, two-week holiday available to an island off of Tunisia, called Kerkennah. It really seemed idyllic with its white sandy beaches and turquoise sea.

This is how I started the conversation up with Andy, 'You know I was keen on going to Australia for a year but I knew I couldn't do it. Then you suggested I go for a month but then I never went? Well would you be ok with me going on holiday to Tunisia, with Jaz, for a couple of weeks?'

To my surprise, Andy agreed to my vacation. He even suggested I could take his Nikon camera with me. Apparently, it was a good one, I didn't know, I didn't know anything about cameras. I was just pleasantly surprised that Andy had accepted my vacation so readily, I guessed he knew it would give him the opportunity to go out drinking every night, uninterrupted. Perhaps he needed a break from me too.

Soon enough the holiday was booked and paid for. A few weeks passed and then I met Jaz for the charter flight at London Gatwick airport. We were excited to see one another, it'd been a while. She still looked the same, pretty with olive skin, big brown eyes, and dark brown hair. Her character full of positivity and enthusiasm.

We flew to a city called Sfax, where my eyes were opened-up to a whole new and exotic world. As the flight came in to land, I squashed my face up to the window. 'Wow' the palm trees were in abundance and the houses looked so strange, built-in squares with courtyards in the middle. I could see the sea and miles and miles of sandy beaches. It was only April but the weather was warm, far too warm for my jeans and denim jacket outfit.

We were mobbed, by local men, as we left

the airport for our transfer bus. 'Hello English' 'Pretty English' 'Kevin Keegan' 'Margaret Thatcher' Michael Jackson.' My attention was constantly diverted as they called out English words and names. I guess they called out in several different languages. I guess I was an obvious fish out of water.

One Tunisian guy grabbed my case and took it directly to the coach for me. 'Oh, thank you' I said, although I was a little confused as I was perfectly capable of carrying it myself.

'Give me one Dinar' he said, with his hand cupped under my nose.

'Oh, I don't have any Tunisian money yet, I only have traveller's checks' I replied.

'Give me English money' He continued.

'Jen, just ignore him and get on the bus!' Jaz interjected.

I got into a bit of a perplexed fluster but I did as I was told. Jaz had much more experience of traveling abroad than I did. She'd back-packed all over India by herself and she'd loved it. I didn't like my first impression of this foreign land but Jaz said it was all part of the experience and the adventure.

We were transported to a boat which took us across the sea to the Islands of Kerkennah. Then another coach journey to our hotel which was called 'The Grand.' The hotel didn't look very grand but the scenery was truly spectacular!

The dry heat really hit me as we disembarked the coach. And I noticed that we were surrounded by palm trees. I detected the fishy smells of the sea combined with exotic mixed spices. I could hear strange music and singing in a foreign tongue, which I guessed was Arabic. All my senses were set on fire and I suddenly felt so alive, so excitable and so free!

We spent two weeks on the island, sunbathing and swimming in the hotel pool and the sea. While evenings were spent in the bar where we were given a lot of attention by the brown-skinned, young local men. We chatted and got friendly with several of them and after a couple of days, they all knew our names. Two good-looking hotel workers made their moves on Jaz and I and it was strange how the other Tunisians backed off. I suppose they had their own rules in their culture. They had their own language too, so Jaz and I really had no clue what was going on.

We also got to know other English holiday-makers who came to feel like good friends within a very short space of time. The hotel was isolated and this caused us to spend a lot of time together and to know each-other quickly. The atmosphere was fantastic. I could walk into the dining room by myself and an English couple might invite me to sit with them. The same in the evening, in the bar or on the beach. We knew everyone! It was like having a perfect happy family and community where I felt known, relevant, and important. While living in paradise, where the weather and food was always ideal.

Jaz and I had already been good friends when we'd lived together in Crystal Palace four years back. But we became closer still over those two weeks. We talked a lot. Jaz loved it in Kerkennah, just as much as I did. We both wanted to stay (like children who cry on the last day of their holiday) and I really didn't want to go back to England, I didn't want to live in east London at all and by now, I knew for sure that I no longer wanted to be with Andy. I knew I had to break up with him and I was dreading going back to do it. But what else could I do.

After showering ourselves in our hotel en-suite, our skin smelled of almond after-sun moisturizer. The French-doors, to the balcony, were wide open and a balmy breeze brought in the soft fragrance of Jazmin flowers. We lay on the starched white sheets of our single beds and got chatting.

'We should come back here!' Jaz announced.

'Yeah, maybe next year' I replied, as I shrugged my shoulders in a kind of defeated expression.

'No, I mean, let's go back to England and sort everything out and come back here in a couple of weeks and rent a house. It'll be an amazing adventure!' Jaz said, in her usual upbeat way.

'How am I gonna do that Jaz?' I replied.

'Just do it Jen! Quit that boring job, you don't love Andy so finish with him, get someone to sublet your flat, then buy a ticket and we'll be back here in a couple of weeks and we can rent a house and stay for a couple of months, in this paradise!' Jaz was incredibly persuasive sometimes.

'Oh, I don't know if I can do that Jaz' I said, as I toyed with the fantasy idea.

'Just do it Jen!' Jaz insisted, 'You know you want to.' I did want to. More than anything. But it all seemed so impossible, so risky and difficult. I wasn't just free to go off as Jaz was. I'd have liked to but I couldn't just throw caution to the wind. I was afraid of the likelihood of losing my flat which would lead to homelessness on my return. Or keeping the flat but being unable to pay my rent and utility bills. And then losing the flat. It was my only place of shelter. I knew well, that no one would help me out in dire circumstances. Or if they did help it would only be temporary assistance. And I needed to be extra careful. I had to cling on to what I had. I needed to think long and hard and behave like an adult!

'But should I really quit a secure job which pays my rent and bills? You know subletting the flat could be a bit risky' I uttered.

'Stop being so materialistic Jen' Jaz said. 'Just do what you wanna do and go with the flow, if it feels right, then it probably is right! God you're just so screwed up that you're ignoring your own wants and needs. You need to live your life and be free!'

The following day, we said goodbye to our new friends and left the islands. The boat took us to the port of Sfax where a coach awaited to give us a short ride to the airport. I was gutted to be leaving and I was just dreading going back to Andy. But that dread made me feel so much guilt. An English tune was playing, on the coach radio, which really affected me because the music was just so soulful and sad.

'Sorry, is all that you can say'

'Years gone by and still'

'Words don't come easily'

'Like sorry, like sorry'

I was thinking about how aggressive Andy had been towards me. How he'd looked with his bloodshot red eyes while foaming at the mouth. And then the flowers and the huge box of chocolates with the idyllic happy family scene-picture on the box. And how he'd made the flat so luxurious. And how Mandy had stopped harassing me since Andy had lived with me. I felt so confused. I cared about Andy. I felt sorry for him. I now realised that he was an alcoholic for sure and maybe his behaviour wasn't really his fault. Alcoholism is an addiction after all. Maybe I should help him. I felt guilty. I felt scared of his reaction if I told him to leave. I kept saying to myself. 'Oh my God, how am I gonna get out of this situation!'

'Forgive me'

'Is all that you can say'

The music continued as we arrived at Sfax Airport and the tears were rolling down my cheeks in anticipation of my return to the concrete jungle in England's capital city.

Chapter 6

Staying

On my return, the fragrance of Andy's aftershave hit me as soon as I entered the flat. He'd obviously shaved and showered in anticipation of my return and his scent was somewhat overwhelming. I felt sick from traveling and his stench but I put on a brave face and fake smile. Andy knew immediately that something was wrong. I just couldn't act normal. I guess he had a feeling, while I was away, that we were close to breaking up.

I'd intended not to start on the subject of us, immediately, but he could feel the bad vibes and there was no way around it.

'Hey' I said, as I entered the living room and Andy stood up to great me.

Where I would have normally kissed him on the lips, I instinctively gave him my cheek by reflex. I clocked that knowing look in his eyes and, although I was tired from traveling, I thought I better just say it now. I was always the honest type, I couldn't live with fakery, not even for a minute of peace. We sat down opposite one another and he had that look of nervous anticipation, I suppose we both did.

'Erm, I don't know how to say this but, erm, I've been thinking about us and our situation, while I was away and I think, erm, I'm sorry but we should break up,' I blurted out.

'No, come on Jen, we can work it out' Andy demanded.

'I can't,' I insisted. 'I'm sorry.'

'Don't be silly, you've just got the post-holiday blues. I've been thinking about refurbishing the kitchen, how'd you want it?' He continued.

'Andy it's no good, I just don't feel right anymore, I'm sorry, I'm gonna go traveling with Jaz. We're gonna go back and live in Kerkennah for a couple of months' I said.

'I'm gonna quit drinking' He insisted.

'No' I shook my head. 'I mean yes, please stop drinking, for your own sake. But I'm sorry, we're finished. I can give you some time to find somewhere else to live. Obviously, I'm not gonna throw you out on the street. And you can take whatever household items that you need or we can just split everything, divide it fifty-fifty straight down the middle' I continued.

Then I looked at Andy and he was crying.

'Please Jen, I'm sorry, I'm sorry I lost my temper in the past, it won't happen again, I just love ya so much, you're my world!' He sobbed.

Next day I was back at work and I called Jaz from the office. 'It's gonna take me a bit longer than a couple of weeks to get things sorted here. I'm having a terrible time with Andy' I said. 'He's just so distraught and I feel awful.

'You still up for going back to Kerkennah though yeah?' Jaz questioned.

'Yeah of course I am' I insisted. I was up for living in paradise, of course I was. But now I was back in east London, paradise seemed a million miles away. And the fantasy idea appeared a difficult and unlikely reality.

'Where there's a will, there's a way Jen!' Jaz persevered, on a day when I felt I just couldn't go through with it all. 'Come on Jen, don't back out on this, make it happen, don't let me down now!'

'Ok, I'll try,' I replied. 'Ok, alright, I'll do it, I'll somehow make it happen'

After much hesitation, eventually, I handed in my one month's notice to quit my job. Jaz and I planned to go off on our trip the day after my last working day, which would be during the first week of June. Because we were now independent travellers, we bought a two-month 'scheduled' return flight which would go from London Heathrow to Tunisia's capital, Tunis. And I started asking around at work to try and find someone to sublet the flat, for while I was going to be away. Which really concerned me as I worried that Mandy would tell the council and I might lose the flat. But I was desperate to escape for a while and now prepared to take the risk.

'Sorry to ask this Andy, but have you been looking for another place to live?' I asked, 'any luck?'

'Look, you need someone ere to pay the rent and watch the flat and I need somewhere to live, so why don't I just stay ere for another couple a month and then I'll leave when you get back from Tunisia' Andy reasoned. 'It would really help me a lot, if I didn't ave the stress of aving to find somewhere else to live on top of breaking up with ya.'

Well, I thought to myself, how that idea did seem to make sense, it would help Andy out a lot and I'd feel less guilty about the whole situation. Also, it would save me having to find and trust someone else with the flat and all my stuff. Andy knew how to take care of everything and he knew how everything worked. The boiler had recently become a bit temperamental but Andy knew how to hit it in the right place, to get it going again when it clicked off. I couldn't be sure others would manage to deal with it and all the other little quirks in the flat. And the council would always take ages if I got onto them to fix anything.

Mandy was used to seeing Andy about and she

might not even realise that I wasn't still there too, if he stayed, instead of some new face. This situation would surely prevent me being reported to the council. But then again, maybe it was better to make a clean break from Andy? Perhaps it wasn't sensible to let my ex-boyfriend stay. Then I heard the song in my head which Jaz and I had heard and sang so many times.

'She's got a ticket,'

'I think she's gonna use it,'

'Think she's gonna fly away.'

I thought about it for a moment, then made a snap decision. I told Andy that he could stay in the flat. He knew my return date and I made it clear that he should be out before then.

'Oh, that's great, you can borrow me camera again if you want,' Andy said. 'Now at least I don't av ta stress about finding somewhere else ta live right away.' He seemed so relieved and I felt much better too.

Everything was sorted. I'd quit my job, I'd finalised the breakup with Andy, my bags were packed and tickets bought and paid for. I was finally going to go off with a good friend, to an idyllic place, to have a Tunisian adventure. To live a little. I was looking forward to it but at the same time, I felt sorry for Andy and I had to watch myself with him.

We were still sleeping together, in the double bed,

and soon after we'd agreed the new upcoming arrangement, Andy tried his luck with me and I again refused him. So, he started touching himself until he reached a climax all over the side of the bed and the carpet. I didn't dare put the light on to clean up his mess so I pretended to sleep and vowed to clean up in the morning. As he went off to work next day I scrubbed and cleaned the mess he'd made. I had a mixture of feelings, shock, disgust and sympathy and I didn't know what to make of this behaviour. He'd made the flat so luxurious and yet he would do such a piggish thing. I felt sick with the mess and the stress of it all.

The last few days were really difficult. Andy was heartbroken about me going off. He was drinking heavily and directing a lot of anger towards me. From time to time, he'd try his luck with me and I felt sorry to refuse but at the same time I had no interest in him, in that way, anymore. He actually repulsed me in that way now and I needed to send a clear message anyway. So, I did refuse. He obviously felt rejected but it was all I could do. The sooner he accepted that we were over, the sooner he would seriously start looking for his own place. I surmised.

Chapter 7

Almost Idyllic

Jaz and I met up at Heathrow airport, rather than Gatwick. This was because we had a two-month return scheduled flight, rather than a charter flight with all the holiday makers. Jaz said that this meant that we were both real travellers now. It was peak holiday season but we flew with businessmen and ordinary Tunisians, to the capital of Tunis. A long train journey then took us directly south, to the second largest city in Tunisia - Sfax.

Although the local language was Arabic, we (being of obvious European completion) were spoken to in French. Neither language was of any use to me at the time and I hardly recognised the difference. Luckily Jaz (who'd completed a private-school education) understood some French and so I relied upon her to get us to our destination. We made it to the port of Sfax and then over on the boat to the tropical islands of Kerkennah.

Our Tunisian friends were delighted to see us again, as we checked into the Grand Hotel. We would stay there for a couple of nights while we asked around for ideas on where we could rent a house. It was June and the weather was scorching hot! And it was just great to be back.

The main town of Kerkennah was called Remla. There were no hotels or tourists there but a house was available for rent at a very reasonable price. We were told about it by the hotel waiter, called Ahmed. He was the one who'd liked me and had made a beeline for me when Jaz and I had first shown our faces on the islands, a couple of months back. He took me on the back of his moped, to see the house, while Jaz followed behind with her guy, Hamza. At one point the two mopeds were side by side. As the Tunisians spoke to one another in Arabic, Jaz and I chatted in English.

'This is such fun!' I shouted.

'Yeah, lets remember this moment right Now, forever!' Jaz said. And we always did.

The house was located on the far side of Remla. It was large, built in a square, with four rooms around the edges. There was a kitchen-dinner and a huge shower room. But the best thing was the courtyard in the middle. We could sunbath naked there if we wanted to and no one would see us. Not that I was too much into sunbathing as I burnt so easily. While Jaz was already a golden brown.

We paid out for a month's rent, which was ridiculously cheap by comparison to London prices. It was about half the price of rent I paid for my council flat. And I was splitting that with Jaz!

Then we chose our respective bedrooms. Mine was basic, with some simple wooden furniture and a comfortable mattress on the floor. The bedroom door overlooked the central courtyard, as all the rooms in the house did, and the window looked outwards to a sea of palm-trees. It was a truly wonderful aspect.

Jaz and I walked into the local town of Remla to do some food shopping. We purchased fresh, organic vegetables from the market and very free-range eggs from a little shop where hens and a cockerel were squawking and crowing. We came back to the house and cooked vegetable omelettes. We found coffee in a cupboard and made ourselves a cuppa on the stove moka-pot. We laughed and chatted non-stop and it was a kind of idyllic heaven.

Due to my previous life events, I suppose I was traumatised and had a plethora of complex issues which inevitably effected my behaviour. I seemed to have heightened emotions which was great when the emotion was positive. But I could get very upset and angry. Jaz listened and counselled me when my emotions got out of whack. No one really knew or understood what I'd been through or the best cause of action but at least Jaz cared enough to listened and tried her best to advise.

Many of the hotel staff lived in and around the main town of Remla. They went on their mopeds to the touristic area, to work at the Grand. So, during the late mornings, we'd just go out with our swimming bags and other items which we'd require for the day. And we'd easily hitch a ride.

We'd enjoy the company of our Tunisian friends, and different holiday-makers as they came and went from the hotel. And we'd spend our time chatting and walking on the sandy beaches, while the sun was up. Sometimes we'd be invited and take the opportunity of going out on the local wooden fishing boats. Or we might borrow the hotel's bicycles and see what we could find, locally in the touristic area, on the island.

Evenings were usually spent in the hotel bar where a disco blared-out the latest English tunes and Arabic favourites, which we soon came to recognise and enjoy. When the English music stopped and the Arabic music played, most of the holiday-makers would clear the dancefloor and the local men would belly-dance. But it was nothing like my western idea of belly-dancing. Jaz and I tried to emulate their dancing, as did a couple of English holiday-makers. But we practised so much that we really became quite good at it. We also started to learn some basic Arabic words and French. At the end of the evening, we'd get a lift back to our traditional Tunisian house on the other side of Remla.

One day we went out from our house into the centre of Remla, as usual, to pick up some fresh vegetables and other supplies. We were wearing shorts and tea-shirts but nothing too revealing.

We were aware of the local girls dressing very modestly and we didn't want to offend anyone by showing off too much skin. It was a completely different culture to ours after all. But although our intention was to blend in, we definitely looked like tourists, especially me with my big sunglasses and wide-brimmed, floppy sunhat.

We noticed that the local police were hanging around but we didn't pay too much attention to them. Then suddenly they were right behind us and speaking to us in French. I wasn't sure what was happening but Jaz said that they wanted us to go into the police station with them and that we didn't have a choice about it.

The main policeman sat at his office desk with a sullen look on his face while another two stood staring us up and down. The main guy was talking and almost shouting while Jaz and I attempted to interpret what he was saying. I didn't have a clue what was happening and soon quit trying. I just stood there nervously shrugging my shoulders and shaking my head, every time he bellowed. The main policeman soon realised that he had no chance of getting me to understand much. So, he directed all of his attention entirely on poor Jaz.

'Aetani Passport' he said, with both of his hands held out in our directions.

Well, that was an international word which everyone understood. We knew that everyone must carry an identification card or, in our case, passports. And luckily Jaz and I had followed the law and both always had our passports on us. We handed them over for inspection and they were promptly checked and handed back to us as the questioning continued.

After about half an hour of broken French and Arabic conversation, we were set free. As we exited the police station, Jaz explained everything of which she'd understood.

The policeman had asked why we were in Kerkennah and more specifically, why we were renting a house near Remla. They'd seen us on the back of several different men's mopeds and they'd reached the conclusion that we were giving sexual favours to the locals, for money! Jaz had insisted that we were not doing such things but she was unsure if they'd accepted that. They just couldn't comprehend what we were doing there otherwise. As far as they were concerned, if we were tourists then we should be staying in the hotel Grand in the tourist area. Why would two young women rent a house in Remla and stay for so long? Why did we accept so many lifts on different men's mopeds? To the police, it was obvious - that we were prostitutes.

Jaz had tried to explain that it would be far too expensive for us to stay in the hotel for two months. But the policeman had said something along the lines of 'You are English, you are rich.'

Then Jaz had tried to explain that we wanted to feel that we were experiencing the Tunisian way of life by living in amongst the locals. But her French hadn't been good enough to articulate this. She'd gotten frustrated as the policeman told us that we were not permitted to be seen on more than one guy's moped in the future. We were allowed one 'boyfriend' each 'only' and if we were seen on the back of other guys' bikes, we could be arrested for the crime of prostitution.

We were so relieved to be released from the police station that we laughed about the prospect of being labelled 'prostitutes.' But deep down, we were both a little shaken-up by the experience of the day and neither one of us wanted to end up in a Tunisian jail!

Now we had a problem. Our official 'boyfriends' couldn't always give us a lift to and from the tourist part of the Islands. Jaz's guy didn't even live near Remla. To get to the Grand hotel from Remla, was about five miles and just about impossible to walk, especially in the heat, which was constant during the day-light hours. In the evening it was pitch-dark and there were wild packs of dogs to watch out for too. The hotel Grand had rentable push-bikes but Remla was outside of the allowable range to cycle them. There were very few taxis available and we were likely to get ripped-off by unscrupulous taxi-drivers if we took them anyway. There was an irregular bus service but the stop was far from being a convenient drop off point at the tourist end. And the prospect of struggling back and forth on these smelly old vehicles would put us off from bothering going to the tourist area altogether.

So, with our police-ban on accepting lifts, we were now locked-down in Remla. I didn't find this scenario so bad and was prepared to accept it. I loved the house and as Ahmed lived in Remla too, I often spent time with him. And I enjoyed trips to the market. Ideally, I wanted to be able to go to the touristic area too but I could live without it, if I had to. But Jaz wanted to quit the Remla house altogether. She wanted to move to another house closer to the tourist area and similarly, a more convenient location to Hamza. She said we would be able to borrow hotel bicycles and be totally independent if we could get accommodation in the nearest village to the tourist zone. This did make sense but I was loathe to the idea of leaving our lovely Remla house.

Jaz was forthright, in character, and insisted that we move to the village closest to the tourist zone, for our second month on the islands. The village was called Ouled Yaneg and Jaz asked our Tunisian friends about possible houses to rent there. But nothing was available. I said that perhaps we should just stay where we were in Remla but Jaz had made her mind up.

Eventually, the hotel receptionist, who was a very

helpful man, told us about an old house which no one had occupied for over fifty years and the locals said was 'haunted.' It was hundreds of years old and in the village of Jaz's preferred location. The house could only really be described it as - a complete and utter ruin.

A big wooden door, with a huge castle-type key, led us into the remains of an ancient mess. There was no scullery or kitchen left, no bathroom and no running water. A hole in the ground excuse for a toilet, occupied a space near a water-well in a rubble and weeded old courtyard. The roof of the house was missing except for over two of the rooms, our potential bedrooms. There was no electricity. The place was a treacherous disaster zone. And I really didn't want to stay there.

'Come on Jen, it'll be fun!' Jaz insisted. 'It'll be like camping.'

Having been forced to live in squats to avoid the elements, during my latter teenage years, the last thing I was up for was living in a derelict house which was 'like camping!' Actual camping, in a tent, would have been better than this place. I wanted to spend our second month in the Remla house but Jaz was adamant. She was done with the Remla house. So, we paid a very cheap month's rent, next to nothing really, up front for the old ruins and moved our stuff there.

The locals thought we were completely mad.

They couldn't understand why two young English women would actually choose to live in those conditions, 'Inti Mahboula!' Our friends would say to us, which is Arabic for 'You're crazy women!'

My 'room' had ancient Arabic calligraphy on the walls, which probably would have been behind glass and in a museum in England. The walls were all crumbling and creatures' nests were in the cracks. Big black beetles would crawl over me during the night as I tried to sleep on the wooden floor without even a mattress. I was unnerved and didn't want to sleep there alone.

Jaz thought the situation was ok. She showed me how to draw the water up from the well and to throw it down the toilet-hole to flush it. We found a huge vessel in, what would have been, the original scullery-kitchen and lifted it to the open courtyard. It was like a giant tagine. Jaz filled it with cold water, drawn up from the deep well. We waited a few minutes for the heat of the sun to warm the water. Then I stripped naked and sat in there to take my makeshift bath. Afterwards, we threw the water onto the weeds and then drew more fresh water for Jaz to do the same. I guessed this was part of the adventure which Jaz craved but it wasn't what I wanted.

After a few miserable days of fighting against my new living conditions and attempting to change back, I accepted our new situation. It's funny, no uncanny, how humans can adjust to just about anything. And I guess, in some ways, I was able to adjust to this kind of squalor, quicker than most.

I had to admit that the ruin-house was in a much more convenient location for getting to the hotel. In the mornings, we would go to a local café, full of local men, and get our coffee. 'Sabah alkhayr mahboula' the voices would call out, which means - good-morning crazy women. But we supposed it was said in jest and we soon accepted our new nick-names. Well, we had little choice about it anyway. Then we'd cycle back and forth at our leisure, to the hotel Grand, on our borrowed hotel bicycles.

It soon transpired that there was another English woman living in Ouled Yaneg. A slight, blonde haired, older woman of sixty years, had been renting a house in the village for a year or so. I was introduced to Suzie one evening at the hotel and got along with her right away. And she invited me to visit her at her rented villa.

Next day I went to visit Suzie. I discovered that in recent years she'd come through a messy divorce and had come out to Kerkennah initially on holiday. Then shortly afterwards, she'd rented the house to recuperate and recover from her life's disasters. She lived in an idyllic two bedroomed villa with windows which directly overlooked the balmy sea. Suzie had no intension of ever leaving the island. Other than having to pop out of the country every three months to have her passport stamped to satisfy visa requirements.

Rumour had it that Suzie had fallen in love with a twenty-four-year-old hotel waiter, on her first visit to the island. I guessed this 'relationship,' coupled with her recent divorce, had inspired her to make the move out to the island. It turned out that the young man had used her and fleeced her for a lot of presents and financial gifts before they'd split. Now most of the locals just considered her a silly old fool and paradise had turned out to be a lonely place. Still, she planned on remaining there for the rest of her life.

I felt quite attached to Ahmed. He couldn't speak much English but he'd learned (before I came along) to say, 'I love you' and 'Very, very love' Which I thought was extremely cute. I guess I fell in love with the island, the weather and the culture which was mixed in with my feelings for Ahmed. Jaz's guy was called Hamza and he worked as an entertainer in the hotel. His English was much better than Ahmed's. While both were very good looking.

Unfortunately, it transpired that Hamza had a 'Real' English girlfriend who came back out to the island around the time that we moved to Ouled Yaneg and poor Jaz got ditched. Jaz also had to pretend nothing had gone on between the two of them so as he didn't get into big trouble with his real girlfriend who was also English. She'd worked the previous summer as the hotel holiday representative and was on her way back to work again. Jaz and I were both convinced that Hamza was such a nice guy that we did keep our mouths shut at the hotel, for his sake.

The situation was pretty upsetting for Jaz, she genuinely loved Hamza. In all the years I knew her before and after Tunisia, I never saw her love any other guy like she loved him. And I think in some way Hamza loved Jaz too, I'm sure I saw it in his hazel eyes. But he was in some kind of a pickle that he couldn't get out of.

We would sometimes watch departing guests getting onto their coaches. As they left, the male hotel workers would wave them off with tears in their eyes. Then they'd be full of excitement and smiles as the new coachload of tourists came in. I hadn't seen Ahmed doing this but it did make me question my situation with him. I'd convinced myself that he truly loved me and I believed that that was the reason why he was so keen to come to England. But sometimes I had niggling doubts as he occasionally behaved as though he didn't much care for me at all. But I told myself that this was just cultural differences i.e., men just behaved differently in Tunisian culture.

One evening I was chatting with Suzie, in the hotel bar and she was trying to convince me that Ahmed was only after me for the prospect of getting into England. I really didn't want to hear this and almost refused to listen at that moment. But as the evening went on, I realised that she was right. I was just being used and Suzie had put herself in the motherly position of telling me the hard truth, at the risk of me never speaking to her again. She'd told me I was being taken for an absolute fool (she admitted to knowing a lot on that subject) and eventually I accepted it to be true. All the little signs had been there right from the start. I hadn't liked those signs so I'd simply ignored them or made excuses for them. But I believed Suzie cared about me and didn't want to hurt me with the truth but felt she had to. So, when I popped out onto the terrace for some air and caught Ahmed flirting with one of the new arrivals, I decided that that was it and our situation was over. He wasn't bothered, there were plenty more fish in the English Channel, plenty more girls where I came from.

A week before Jaz and I were due to fly back to England, I telephoned Andy, from the hotel Grand. The nice receptionist, called Mahmood, kindly let me make the call for free from the reception telephone. I hoped Andy wouldn't answer at all, this would make me pretty sure that he'd moved out from my flat as agreed. But he did answer.

'Hello?' Andy spoke.

'Hi Andy it's me, Jen.' I began.

'Alright Jen.' Andy replied.

'How're you? Is everything alright at the flat?' I

continued.

'Yeah, fine, I've paid the rent and everyfing.' He spoke.

'Great, thanks and have you found somewhere else to live now?' I questioned.

'No, I'm still ere' he said.

'Well, ya know we can't live together don't ya?' I spoke.

'Why not?' He replied.

'Because we're not together anymore and you agreed that you would leave before I got back' I said.

'You got another bloke or somefing!' Andy said, as he started to raise his voice.

I was exasperated. Andy had promised to move out by now and here he was, still at the flat and demanding I give him answers to questions which were now nothing to do with him. I had a feeling that if I said I had another bloke, Andy might get really angry. But this white lie might finally make him give up on me and leave the flat. At this point he still seemed to have no intention of leaving and I had to get him out somehow. I didn't really have another bloke but I said, 'Yeah that's right I've got a new boyfriend'

'I'm gonna burn this fucking flat darrn!' Andy screamed.

'Oh my God, please just leave, just find somewhere else to go!' I pleaded.

'You gonna bring ya new boyfriend ere are ya,' Andy continued.

Well, the true answer was 'no' but I honestly thought that saying 'yes' was my only chance of getting Andy to accept that we were finished and to make him move out - so I made a snap decision and I said, 'Yes that's right, I've got a boyfriend and he's coming back with me!'

'I'm gonna burn this fucking flat to the fucking grarnd!' he shouted.

I didn't want to hear this. I didn't know what else to say. I wanted him to stop mouthing off. I wanted him to shut up, so I slammed the phone down; I couldn't take anymore. I put my hands to my head and cried, 'Oh God, help me God!'

Sleeping had been difficult since we'd moved into the ruin house in Ouled Yaneg. But now, I was so stressed out, it was almost impossible to sleep at all.

Chapter 8

Concrete Echo

A few days after that telephone conversation with Andy, I said goodbye to Suzie. We'd exchanged addresses and agreed that she would come and visit me in London, someday. As well as writing to one another, we could also keep in touch by telephone. She had my number and I could always catch her most weekend evenings, if I wanted to call her, at the Grand.

We said goodbye to all of our friends and left the Kerkennah Islands. I held back my tears through Sfax and all the way to Tunis airport. Next, we were on the flight to England and it suddenly seemed just a heartbeat of time since we'd first arrived in Tunisia, two months ago.

In no time at all we were back on English soil. Jaz's parents and younger brother drove all the way from Bristol to welcome Jaz home, at London Heathrow airport. They hadn't seen her for two months and were obviously genuinely excited and full of love for her. They were hugging and kissing her at the airport arrivals area, while I just stood there smiling like a lemon. Then Jaz's mum noticed me just standing there awkwardly and tried to include me in their celebration greetings. She obviously felt sorry for me and gave me a quick kiss on the cheek. Bless her, what more could she do. Then the four of them headed off, arms linked, in the direction of the car-park, for their journey home. With my green eyes, I stood and watched Jaz and her family walking off together.

Then I started my way back to east London's concrete jungle, on public transport, alone. To say I was filled with dread, at the prospect of returning to the flat, would be an understatement. I'd hardly slept in the preceding days, due to anxiety and pure fear. I had so much swishing around in my head. Breaking up with Ahmed, saying goodbye to Suzie and Jaz, leaving a tropical paradise to live in east London, being jobless, having no one, having bills to pay. But worst or all, the imminent problem of dealing with a heartbroken and potentially violent man, on my arrival at the flat. I dreaded confrontation with Andy, I feared what he might be capable of. But then again, maybe he'd just accepted that we were finished and quietly left. At this point anything was possible.

Oh, how I wished I had a friend or a loving relative beside me, as I put my key in the door of the flat and turned it. The door slowly creaked open and all was deathly quiet. As I stepped inside, my shoe landed on the solid concrete floor and there was a noticeable and obvious echo. The corridor carpets and underlay had all gone and all that was left were the spiky wooden strips which the carpet should normally be attached to. I stood, in shock, for a moment. The hallway telephone table was missing. All I could hear was silence and my own stressed breathing. I dropped my travel-case and hand luggage and carefully entered the living room. It was completely bare. Devoid of all furniture, carpets and curtains. Except for the telephone apparatus, Andy had taken the lot! He'd cleared the place out!

It was the same situation in the bedroom. Everything was gone, except for my clothes and a few old sheets and towels. Then I noticed a large note pinned on the wall. It was a photocopied printout which read 'Wanker of the Week' in large printed letters. Then smaller letters read - 'This award goes to....... 'And then handwritten, in Andy's own handwriting..... 'Jennifer Ashcroft.'

As I stood there feeling perplexed and shocked at the absurdity of the situation, the telephone started ringing on the living room floor. 'Hello' I said. But no one spoke and I immediately knew it was Andy. He obviously wanted to know if I was back, he wanted to imagine how I looked on seeing all the furniture and luxury gone.

All I could think of was to call Jaz. 'Jaz, Andy's taken everything, I don't even know how he's done it but he's cleared the place out, carpets an all!' I cried.

'Shit Jen, oh that's shocking. Oh well at least he's gone yeah, at least you can rest in peace now. Listen we've not long got in and mum's about to dish up dinner so I'll talk to you another time, ok? You'll be alright though yeah, chat soon yeah.'

I hastily delved into my hand-luggage bag and located my tooth brush and paste. I gave my teeth a good clean, as if it was the most important thing I could possibly do at this moment in time. Then I filled myself up on tap water. I was exhausted so I placed two towels down on the concrete floor. I put a sheet on top of the towels. I folded another towel in the shape of a makeshift pillow. I turned the harsh overhead light off then lay down and pulled another couple of towels over me as blankets.

Then the telephone rang and I got up to answer and again no one spoke. And again, and again until I unplugged the telephone. I was exhausted but my hips ached from the cold hard floor and I tossed and turned, trying to get comfortable. I had the feeling that Andy would turn up. That he would bang on the door, at any moment, or put a brick through one of my windows. I felt that sickness you feel when you've been traveling all day. I had only the remnants of the plastic airplane meal still lining my empty stomach.

I imagined how Jaz had sat around the dining-room table with her family this evening. They were obviously thrilled with her return. She'd have eaten her favourite meal, freshly prepared by her mum. And everyone would've been fascinated to hear of her Tunisian island adventures. They would have laughed and chatted throughout meal-time and then retired upstairs. By now I guessed that Jaz would be tucked up in her freshly-made double-bed and fast asleep. It was difficult not to taste a bitterness in my dry mouth. As I lay there on that cold floor, I tried hard not to let jealousy get under my skin as my self-pity overwhelmed me.

I'd broken Andy's heart but I didn't deserve what he'd done to me. It was so unfair of him to literally take everything from the flat. He must have taken the carpets directly to the dump. As they were shaped to fit the floors of my flat, they wouldn't be any use anywhere else. He'd gone to the extreme effort of peeling them off the floors, purely to spite me.

I felt afraid that Andy would turn up to kill me and no one would even attempt to save me. Mandy (upstairs) probably wouldn't even call the police if she heard my screams nowadays. And I might not have time to plug the telephone back in, to call them myself! That worried me so I got up and plugged the phone back in. Then I was on my guard all night, looking out for the changes in the shadows at the windows. I hardly slept for worrying and tossing and turning.

Soon it was daylight, so I got up and rummaged around at the back of the kitchen cupboards. I found a few non-perishable items there and made myself a black-tea. Tea was not nice without milk but better than nothing at all. I reminded myself that things could always be worse. I reminded myself of these words, 'I cried when I couldn't afford new shoes, until I saw a man with no legs.' (That's the sort of thing mum used to say to us - all her little sayings always stuck in my head and came back to me at times like this.) Then I made my way to the local police station. A crime of theft had surely been committed.

At the police station, I explained how everything had been taken from the flat by my ex. Everything! 'It's so unfair!' I declared. The policeman agreed but he said, there was nothing he could do as this was a 'civil matter' and not a 'police matter.' I should definitely get a solicitor to sort it all out, he said. Then, regarding my fear of being attacked or worse, I should definitely call the emergency services on 999 if Andy turned up at the flat. This gave me little to no comfort. If Andy were to turn up, he could get into the flat within seconds. Of course, I would change the locks but he could come through the single-glazed windows in ten seconds flat, if he really intended to get me.

There was a solicitor's office, just above a cake-shop, on my way back to the flat. I walked in and up the stairs and managed to get an appointment right away. New clients were apparently given priority. The male solicitor listened intently and wrote down all of the details. He suggested that he would now write a strong letter to Andy, explaining the seriousness of his actions. He would threaten to take things further i.e., court, unless the sum of £2000 was paid to me to cover replacement costs of carpets, curtains, some essential furniture, and some electrical goods as a minimum. For this, the solicitor would require £200 from me and Andy's new address.

Well of course I didn't know where Andy was staying but I suspected he'd gone to his brother's. And even if he wasn't there, his brother could pass the letter onto him. I gave the solicitor Andy's brother's address and then I withdrew the £200. I dropped it back to the solicitor's receptionist. Then I paid £50 to a locksmith to have my locks changed. My funds were now very low indeed but if I got the £2000 from Andy, I'd be able to survive. Or if I even got half of that some and a few household items back, I'd be satisfied.

After a miserable week, the solicitor's secretary called me to let me know that the solicitor's letter had been returned, marked 'unknown at this address.' The Solicitor's letter had been stamped with the name of his Law company so obviously neither Andy nor his brother would open it. The secretary said that my solicitor could continue writing letters but this would obviously cost me. I realised that this endeavour would likely be fruitless, so I started to give up.

I then discovered how Andy had removed

everything from the flat. An older neighbour, living opposite, described the scene. A couple of days before my return from Tunisia, a large van 'like a removals van' had pulled up at my flat. Two men, one was Andy and the other (from description) was Scott, had worked 'all day' clearing out my flat. But not everything had gone inside the van. She'd seen several items of 'nice wooden furniture' being taken up the steps to the flat above me.

Andy had pulled an evil kind of clever trick. He'd either sold or given away, our most beautiful items of French-polished furniture, to my vile neighbour, Mandy, who he knew hated me for no apparent reason. Not only would I lose our stuff but I'd lose it to her, of all people.

To be sure my elderly neighbour had gotten her story right, I went upstairs and knocked on Mandy's door. I don't know what I'd have said if she'd have answered and it was probably good that she didn't. She was out and the dog was yapping. I opened the letter-box and peeped through. I could see my beautiful telephone-table in the corridor with Mandy's telephone on top. The edge of my TV cabinet could be seen, just inside her living-room door.

I now knew nothing could be done. It was a most cruel move on Andy's part, which served to obliterate any last feelings of concern which I may have still held for him. I gave up on ever retrieving any items or cash compensation and told my solicitor's secretary that their services were no longer required.

I'd felt terribly sorry for Andy at one point and I'd been overwhelmed with guilt at breaking up with him. But now all the guilt had disappeared because of the actions he'd taken. Prior to him removing everything from my flat, there'd always been a slim chance that we would get back together but now all chances were gone. Even if I had to sleep on the floor, I was relieved that Andy was gone. Better all the luxury was missing than he still being in my life.

Chapter 9

Two Jobs

After my return from Kerkennah, I spent several weeks worrying that Andy would show up to harass or attack me but he never did. And I put that down to him thinking that I might have another boyfriend staying with me. Andy was tough and aggressive towards me but he was chicken when it came to other men.

Andy only tried his luck again with me once more (by telephone) it was a couple of weeks after my return to the empty flat.

'Alright Jen, it's Andy, how are ya?'

'What d'you want?' I questioned.

'I was wondering if you wanna meet up with me, I'll take you out to dinner and we can talk about everything.' He waited for my reply.

'Are you joking? After you took everything from me? You cleared out my flat!' I spoke. 'I came back to nothing!'

'Well, I can help you get it all back, lets meet on Saturday afternoon, in Stratford. We can go round the shopping centre and I'll buy you a new CD player, then I'll take ya to dinner?' Andy said.

'Are you joking?' I repeated, after you took everything!'

Andy's tone changed. 'You must be mistaken, I never took nofin' he lied.

'Alright, bye,' I said as I cut the call.

He called straight back.

'What do you want?' I demanded.

'You've got my camera,' Andy spoke, 'And I need it back, meet me on Saturday ta give it me, I won't cause no trouble, I'll just take ya for a quiet drink.'

'No, I don't have your camera,' I lied. 'I lost it.'

'Well, let's just meet up anyway, what's the harm?' He continued.

Luckily I was completely over Andy and therefore, even though I was lonely and bored on Saturdays, I didn't want to be in the same room as him ever again. So, although I did hesitate for a moment when I pictured a new CD player, it still wasn't difficult to turn his offer down.

'No thanks.' I spoke.

'Well, if you change ya mind, ya know where ta find me, I still drink in the Queen's ed yeah,' He insisted.

'Yeah, that's not gonna happen.' I spoke in a flat tone,'

'Oh bloddy fuck ya then ya fucking sla..'

I cut the call and this time Andy didn't call back. I guess he made his way straight to the pub and knocked back ten pints of lager followed by Vodka shots. That's not an exaggeration, he genuinely and regularly drank that amount. It's sad really. I vowed never to be with a drinker ever again and thankfully, I never heard from Andy again.

By now, all of my funds were exhausted and I was heading into bank-overdraft. My rent was due and my utility bills were all overdue. I spent my time alone in the almost empty flat. I missed the golden sunshine of Kerkennah as the dreadful English rain lashed down against my single-glazed windows. I put my hands on the glass, like a prisoner and howled out, out of self-pity. I also missed the constant company of my companion, who I thought of as my sister, Jaz. And my substitute mother - Suzie.

I had to find a job to survive but so far, my trips to the local job-centre had been fruitless. So, out of desperation, I called my old boss Ian, to kind of beg for my old job back.

At least Ian sounded pleased to hear my voice, on the other end of the telephone. But unfortunately, he had no vacancies for Clerical Officers. However, if I were willing to face the shame of returning to the office at the lower position of Clerical Assistant, then he could probably arrange it.

Ian insisted that the demotion would likely be temporary and I should be promoted back up to Clerical officer again shortly. I had no choice but to accept.

Within days, I was working back at British Telecom and I was back with my old team. But instead of dealing with correspondence, writing letters and working out bills, I was now just filing and photocopying. For some reason my old team had moved from the fourth floor to the first floor. So, we were now surrounded by different teams although most of my own team were the same as when I'd left almost three months prior. I'd taken the lowest level (office) post in the company and so, of course, I was now on a lower wage than before. But at least I would not fall into rent-arrears or bank-overdraft. As I was used to being frugal, I could just about pay my bills.

However, I was now back in the position of suffering from chronic loneliness. In some ways, going from having the constant company of Jaz, Suzie and an abundance of other friends and acquaintances in Kerkennah, made the return loneliness even worse. I suppose I was depressed and this depression was affecting my interest in life in general. I'd lost all connection to things that used to fascinate me as a child and young teenager and I'd become so pessimistic nowadays. I'd been a creative child, but indulging oneself in creativity is a privilege that only the settled can pursue. By now I'd completely forgotten that I was creative in character. Keeping a roof over my head and surviving grief had been my goals, these past few years.

What a mess, what a crappy mess. My babies, my little lost ones, what life could I have offered them if they'd have survived. I was unsettled, disturbed and I had no extended family or community on hand. What kind of mother would I have become.

My only mission now, was avoiding this appalling loneliness. I was desperate to chat with people and used to stare at my home-telephone and will it to ring. But a watched telephone never rings. I had little drive in me other than the hope of filling my void with the pursuit of finding a suitable life-partner. I'd just sit in the window and watch the birds in the sky, I'd watch the clouds. There was movement out there, there was life. I couldn't see any palm trees but I could imagine them.

I didn't fancy advertising myself in the 'Lonely Hearts column' of the local newspaper. Yes, I was desperate but I didn't want to make it official. I had to keep some level of self-respect, didn't I? I couldn't officially be labelled as a desperado, could I. The only other idea I could come up with, was entering public houses alone, in the hope of meeting the love of my life. But this really wasn't the done thing and no fun at all. It would be embarrassing and difficult. I'd almost certainly get latched onto by the first available guy that spotted me and this would prevent me being able to socialise with anyone else. Then it would be hit and miss as to whether that was a good guy for me or not. That's what had happened with Andy and look how that had turned out!

Then I suddenly had an idea! The thought occurred to me that I should get a second job and work in a pub! Then I'd have every right and reason to go out alone. I'd also have extra cash which would definitely come in handy. With a second job I could easily make up the shortfall from my reduced wages as a clerical assistant. I decided I would make telephone enquiries and call all the pubs in Stratford and the surrounding area. If I had no luck there, I'd try some of the less favourable pubs in Forest Gate.

I was young, female (which gave me priority over males, as most punters were male and preferred female bar-staff) and I already had a little experience of working as a barmaid. These three attributes landed me a job in the first pub I called. A lively pub of my choice. It was a disco-pub called The Charleston, located in-between Forest Gate and Stratford, in the heart of London's east end.

'Been around the world and I I I'

'I can't find my baby'

'I don't know when I don't know why'

'Why he's gone away'

'And I don't know where he can be, my baby'

'But I'm gonna find him'

At first, I was required to work Friday and Saturday evenings only but soon I was being asked to come in on Sunday afternoons and other weekday-evenings too. I could have refused to do so many days and the landlord would have accepted it, if I wanted to just stick with Fridays and Saturdays as originally planned. But home was a lonely place and Mandy was being horrible again. So, I was happy to be out of the flat and working every night and Sunday lunchtimes too. Like this I was flush for cash and I gradually refurnished my flat again, with simple carpets, curtains, furniture and electrical goods. I wanted to better myself in some other way too, so I started taking driving lessons, once a week, on Saturday mornings.

I enjoyed being a barmaid and it turned out that I was good at it. I was sociable, a people-person. I was quick-witted and I wasn't much of a drinker (which is actually a very good thing for bar-staff) And it even turned out that I was good at adding up the cost of drinks in my head. The regular practice made it easy. The landlord said, he considered me an asset.

Chapter 10

Mistake

I was busy with my two jobs. I sat down for most of the day in the office and then I was on my feet, running around at the pub in the evenings and weekends. Two extremes, which was a good thing. I was busy and the bubbly side of my character started to shine through again.

A guy of Indian descent, called Kalvin, worked as a Clerical Officer in my office on the next team to me. I hadn't really noticed him at all, until we kept bumping into each other at the photocopier. I guessed he was orchestrating our random interactions. He was very darked skinned and somewhat mysteriously attractive. I suppose he reminded me of Tunisia in some silly way. Yet his family came from southern India and were devote catholic, which I thought was unusual. His accent was cockney and by the way he dressed he appeared to be as English as I was.

My twenty-fifth birthday was coming up and as soon as Kalvin heard about it, he insisted we should celebrate together on our lunchbreak that day. He kept pushing for it and made arrangements for a small group of us to go to a local pub to celebrate and play pool together. I was pretty good at pool as I'd practised so often in the Eddie and the Queen's Head. They say that being good at pool is a sign of a misspent youth, well I don't know about that. Anyway, one by one I beat all the Asian guys who Kalvin had persuaded to come along with us. They all insisted that they'd only let me win because it was my special day. Anyway, we all had fun and I did enjoy this birthday.

After that, I regularly went to the pub to play pool with Kalvin and the Asian guys. Meena didn't want to come to the pub with us, so I was the only girl but that didn't really bother me. At last, I felt like I was starting to get a social life! We all laughed and joked together but it became clear, early on, that Kalvin was obviously keen on me and I really liked him too.

Meena told me that Kalvin had a fiancée and I asked him all about his situation. It seemed that he'd been betrothed to a girl called Josephine, by his and her parents, several years back. But I got the impression that he wasn't uninterested in actually marrying her. Anyway, she lived on the other side of the world right now. From what he'd told me, it seemed she was not interested in marrying him either. His cockney accent and way of dressing told me that he was as English as I was and if English people don't want to marry each other - they just don't.

Whenever I went to the photocopier, Kalvin would appear next to me and we'd mess around saying stupid stuff and making each other giggle. When Kalvin and I went back to our desks, I could see him, he sat far away from me, on the other team at the other end of the office. His back was facing me but every now and then he'd turn around on his swivel chair and give me a cheeky smile. Then he would turn back and call me on his desk telephone to mine and pretend to have some important query to discuss. Like that we'd sit chatting and laughing like we'd known each other for years.

Are ya working in the Charleston tonight?' He questioned one day.

'Yeah, I work every night don't I' I replied.

'I'm gonna come and see ya tonight,' He continued.

The gossip about our office romance was rife before it even got started.

It was a Friday evening in mid-October and it was closing time when Kalvin turned up all full of enthusiasm and smiles.

'I thought you weren't coming' I said.

'Well, I thought I'd come as you finish off here as I wanted to take you out for dinner, do you fancy an Indian?' We both laughed at that one.

By now I understood Indian food a lot better and

tucked into it rather than the English alternative at the restaurant. Kalvin and I only had eyes for each other and that's when the whirlwind romance really took off.

From thereon in, we were inseparable. We'd chat on the telephone across the office every morning, go to lunch together every lunchtime, either in the upstairs canteen or the public house across the road, with the Asian guys from Kalvin's team. Most evenings Kalvin would sit at the bar of the Charleston, while I was working but he wasn't much of a drinker and I was pleased about that. Then he'd give me a lift home. He'd stay for a while but he never stayed over. He said his parents wouldn't accept him staying out all night which I thought was a bit odd. He was a fully grown man in his mid-twenties after all! But I understand now.

Meena kept warning me, 'Kalvin's engaged you know' but I didn't take much notice. I knew he was into me and not the slightest bit interested in marrying this girl from far, far away.

Christmas was upon us and I was busy at the Charleston while Kalvin was busy going to the Catholic church with his family. I felt frustrated as I still hadn't met them and was getting the impression I never would. It was awkward I guess, because of the irrelevant engagement. And Kalvin said he wasn't allowed to have a white English girlfriend as his parents wouldn't accept it. I guess I was starting to feel like his dirty little secret.

I'd wait and wait for him to pop round and visit me at the flat. He'd always come eventually but I definitely felt like I'd lost control of my heart and the situation in general.

Was I just stupid! Was I just ruled by overwhelming emotion, was I just unlucky, was I cursed, was I responsible for my own demise or were the wolves just uncontrollably drawn to me like bees to honey! Or had I been so well trained, in the art of self-punishment that I just couldn't prevent this repetitive circle. Was this just going to turn out to be more in the way of self-flagellation!

I didn't see much of Kalvin as Christmas was a busy time for him. His family were apparently devote catholic and he was obliged to worship in church with them throughout the holiday period. Also, he had many family get-togethers to attend, which I could never be invited to. I cried a lot that Christmas. I worked, in both of my jobs, as much as I could, to try and keep my mind occupied but I still had to spend Christmas Day alone. Although Kalvin did manage to pop around to visit me in the evening.

Then it was January and Kalvin and I were in the lift, going up to the top floor canteen, at work. That's when it all kicked off.

'Hey I've got the date for my driving test.' I began.

'Josephine's on her way to Heathrow, she's flying right now, we'll be getting married in a few weeks,

I don't want to but I have to' He explained.

I couldn't look at him, I was so disappointed with what he'd just told me. I was so upset but still, when it came to the evening, the mad passionate affair continued. I suppose I was trying to convince him not to go through with the wedding. He didn't love her, he loved me! But with hindsight I realise love had little to do with it. I should have backed off. Well, I should never have got involved with him in the first place. That was my mistake.

Kalvin was stressed, I hear big Asian weddings can be incredibly stressful especially when you don't really know your fiancée or her family. And you don't really want to marry! He was stressed and I guess I was his outlet, right up to the night before the wedding. I'd lost my temper with him that night, I'd lost all control as I begged him not to leave me. My countenance was overly emotional in general but that night was something else.

The day of the wedding was a tough one. In my mind's eye I saw it all. Josephine's stunning white lace dress (her virgin body and face veiled.) The packed-out church, the families dressed in colourful, traditional Indian outfits. Then the laughter at the silver service, five course, afternoon meal. A change of outfit at the evening reception, a red and gold traditional wedding dress - beautiful. The nibbles at the after-party, the bhangra music and English pop songs. I wondered if he thought of me, sitting in the dark in silence -

sitting in the window, home alone.

Then Kalvin and his new wife were away on honeymoon, in the Greek Islands, for three weeks. While he was away, I don't know how I did it but I managed to take my driving test. And I was kind of confident that I'd passed. As far as I was concerned, I hadn't made any mistakes. So, I was shocked when the examiner failed me on 'hesitation.' I'd apparently had several opportunities to pull out of the side road and onto the main road but I'd hesitated which meant a big Fail for me. Having no one to comfort me or encourage me into an immediate retake, I quit my lessons and the money I'd spent was wasted. Assuming myself to be simply a failure and a useless person. It was yet more confirmation that life was pointless.

It was the beginning of April by the day Kalvin returned to the office. I could see his wedding-ring glistening in the raising spring sun as it shined through the office glass. It was that bright yellow, Indian gold, twenty-two carats, pure. I'd just sit there watching the light catch it every now and then. Kalvin had stopped calling me, his back faced me as it always had done but now, he didn't swivel around on his chair anymore. He didn't give me that big smile.

I felt absolutely devastated. And to make matters worse, I was the centre of talk of the office gossip due to my own stupidity at getting involved with someone at work. The Asian men, who I thought of as my friends, had zero sympathy for me. It was all apparently my own fault for throwing myself at an engaged man. Perhaps they were right. I'd thought I'd been friends with them once as we'd often gone to the local pub, at lunchtime to play pool together as a group. Now they weren't even speaking to me. I missed being friends with them on top of losing the relationship with Kalvin. Was I trash, to be used and thrown away like that! Yes, it certainly appeared that way.

Meena was a kind colleague, to me, especially during this time. She understood men, better than I did, probably because she had a loving father, decent brothers and kind uncles. And of course, she understood the mentality of Asian men far better than I ever would. 'Kalvin was always going to marry Josephine you know, there was never any doubt about that. And the guys will always take his side, that's just the way it is.' She told me as my tears dripped down my pale face over repeated lunchtimes. 'Why didn't you listen to me?'

'I would never marry someone if I didn't love them' I spoke.

'Yeah, well he's Asian first and English second and it's all just different rules you know.' She continued, 'Find yourself a nice English guy.'

'Yeah, well I've not been very lucky with English guys either.' I spoke. I felt like a hopeless case.

I had to see Kalvin and his shiny golden wedding-ring all day, every day at work. What kind of fool was I? I was now even afraid to risk another relationship. But without someone I felt I was a no one. I was living in a spiritual poverty, devoid of any meaning or purpose to my wasted and purposeless life.

Then there was a reshuffle at work and I was suddenly promoted, back up to Clerical Officer, and moved back up to the fourth floor. At least I no longer could see Kalvin's shiny wedding-ring from my new position. He remained on the first floor, so I guess that was a good thing although I didn't think so at the time. Very occasionally I'd bump into him in the lift but we didn't speak because there really was nothing more to say. And sometimes he'd be in the canteen at the same time as me. But it didn't matter anymore.

My new job was pretty boring. I was on, what was called, the new Call-Reception unit. I literally just sat and took calls all day, every day. But there were two good things, one, I was now a Clerical Officer again and two, I sat opposite my favourite colleague - Meena.

Chapter 11

High hopes

It was 1990 and, as well as my office job, I continued to work at the Charleston most evenings and on weekends. I passed the evening of my twenty-sixth birthday in the pub, which wasn't a bad place to celebrate. And eventually the pain and grief of losing Kalvin, and the awkwardness of my day job in the aftermath of the affair, began to fade.

I decided to work on 'thinking positive.' Money-wise I was now doing ok. I thought about my mother's dying wish for me to own my own home one day. And I decided to apply to buy my council flat under Thatcher's Right to Buy Scheme. Life's what you make it, isn't it?

A group of six young, white-English guys were regulars at the Charleston. They would always chat and flirt with me while I was serving their drinks from behind the circular bar. They were local, cockney lads who apparently played in a Sunday league football team together. But they'd known each-other from schooldays. I found them really entertaining and hilariously funny. They used to all fight for my attention in a kind of joking way, but many a true word is spoken in jest.

This group apparently liked to smoke a bit of the old whacky-backy, the landlord had noticed the strong-smelling smoke on every occasion, when the guys were in the public house. And he'd worked out, it was them, by a process of elimination. But the landlord had only politely asked them to stick to 'cigarettes only' while on the premises. He hadn't wanted to be too harsh as they might take their business elsewhere. They were regular big-spenders and therefore valued clientele. I suppose the effects of the cannabis, combined with the alcohol, always added to their comical behaviour. But although there was a constant odour when they were in the public house, to me, the guys were like a breath of fresh air. One of these guys was called Ritchie. He was tall and good looking with bright blue eyes and he was intelligent and funny. At twenty-six, he was the same age as myself.

Ritchie was leaning up against the bar one night, telling me that his mate (who'd shown a lot of interest in me) was married with three kids. But this turned out to be untrue. It was all just jokes and banter and a way of putting me off of his friend. When his friend found out what Ritchie had told me, they started play-fighting. It was all very entertaining and diverting for me.

Ritchie seemed everything I was looking for in a man. Although he'd apparently disappointed his parents. He was a clever guy and had studied A-levels but had dropped out of high-school as the going got tough. He could have easily gone to university and gone on to become an accountant or solicitor but he'd not bothered. He was now working as a delivery van-driver. He was happy enough with the driving-job for the time being. He lived in local Stratford with his parents and like that he didn't have to take any responsibility in life. He also owned and drove a flashy sports car which I supposed he afforded by having free accommodation. Ritchie was the first person I ever knew with a mobile telephone.

Looking back, I think Ritchie's priorities were - having fun with his friends, playing Sunday league football, and chatting me-up on a regular basis. Living at home with his parents afforded him the freedom to mess around and just enjoy the last years of his extended youth. He'd had an easy life thus far and his parents had allowed him the privilege of continuing his ongoing teenagerhood.

I was very attracted to Ritchie but I was slightly hesitant about going on a date with him. I was just so hurt and broken. Things were good while he was flirting with me and I was still in control of the situation. I wanted to avoid more pain but I was keen to have love in my life and I thought about him all the time. I knew that I was in danger of getting hurt again. With love comes the risk of pain and once you enter it, it can be a slippery slope.

I even spoke on the phone with Suzie about Ritchie. 'Well, he sounds very nice,' she said, 'but, just be careful, don't go rushing into anything, I don't want you getting hurt again. I don't want you ending up like me.

Eventually, I agreed to go on a date with Ritchie. Which meant I needed to take a night off from working at the pub. I'd become a workaholic of late and just didn't have any free time at all. I was still going to my office job too. All in all, I was working thirteen hours on weekdays, in my two jobs, and eight hours on Saturdays and Sundays. I'd also become obsessed with keeping my flat clean and tidy, which wasn't difficult as I didn't have much clutter and I was hardly home. But if I went to bed thinking I'd left something out of place, such as leaving a teacup in the living room, I'd get up to wash it, dry it and put it in the right place. With hindsight I think all this activity just gave me a superficial purpose in life and distraction from loneliness and my past traumas. A way of retaining some control.

So, I took a Thursday off from my evening job and Ritchie and I went out on a date together. He behaved impeccably, he was entertaining, respectful, and just perfect in every way. I thought he acted like a real gentleman when he dropped me off in a taxi and kissed me on the cheek to say 'Goodnight.' I'd expected him to hint at an invite in for 'coffee' but he didn't, so I felt like he really respected me and I fell for him right away.

I skipped work on the Friday evening and Ritchie and I met up with his friends in another public house. They were asking me how our date had gone and I told them what a gentleman Ritchie had been. 'Oh, the old kiss on the cheek routine!' one of them joked.

'It always works a treat that one' another joined in. They were so funny but not entirely incorrect.

I tried to slow my desire down but it was just so difficult to prevent myself from allowing Ritchie in. We were crazy about each-other. I knew he was serious about me when he introduced me to his parents. That weekend he took me to his house and I fell in love with his parents too. They were just so kind and decent. I felt a warm welcome at their house. But I soon realised that they'd spoiled Ritchie in a literal sense of the word. They'd loved him so much and made his life so comfortable that he'd no need to better himself at all. His mum ran around after him, doing his washing and cooking. She evidently loved him so much, while he was ever so slightly disrespectful towards her with his derogatory side-comments, which he dismissed as 'banter.' I guess he could get away with it. He could have been so much more than what he was but he just had no need to be. Life is truly an ironic tragedy.

'Are you coming home tonight, Ritchie?' His mum questioned as we were about to leave his parents' house.

'No chance' Ritchie replied.

I thought his mum deserved a little more than that simple and abrupt reply but all the same I was content that he just wanted to be with me.

As soon as I'd skipped working a couple of evenings at the pub, it got easier to miss the next evening and the next. Ritchie and I wanted to spend as much time together as we possibly could. He was my priority now, so I quit working at the pub altogether. I had my own flat so it was easy for Ritchie to crash at mine night after night. We were really into each-other so the obvious next step was for him to officially move in with me.

I was surprised at how happy Ritchie's parents seemed when he moved out from the family home. I guess they were worried he never would leave home. Now he'd met a girl they both liked and I had my own flat within a few of miles of them. So, they knew that they could see him often enough. I suppose that seemed a win-win situation for them.

Now when an insecure, repeatedly heartbroken, workaholic female, has a mad, passionate love-affair with a high-school dropout - man-teenager, it's unlikely to be an easy ride but I did have high hopes for me and Ritchie. I believed that if I played my cards right, I could make it work. Ritchie had been allowed to remain immature and I just needed to be patient. But patience was a virtue which I sadly lacked.

Ritchie was serious about us too, he gave me his expensive leather jacket which was soft, black and of the highest quality. It was way too big for me but I appreciated the gesture. I wore it to my office job, all the time, with the sleeves rolled up to make it almost fit.

Then it was Christmas day and Ritchie and I were invited to his parents' house for Christmas dinner, in the afternoon. I was thrilled to think that I could now join this normal, happy family and wouldn't have to spend the festive season alone anymore. I was so excited, over-excited, stressed. I knew that Ritchie's parents liked me but I really put pressure on myself to make a good impression on this day, of all days.

This was the closest I would ever come to the little house on the prairie. Ok it wasn't on a prairie, but it was a little semi detached house with a really good and decent loving family. A family that was keen to welcome me in. What happened next is difficult to explain as I still don't fully comprehend it.

Ritchie and I turned up at his parents' house and his sister-in-law answered the door with her three-year-old daughter in tow. His sister-in-law was animated about meeting me and her daughter was stirred up and hyper. They were full of Christmas cheer. I could smell the roasting turkey and all the Christmas decorations were up in place. Prompted by her mother, the little girl gave me a wrapped gift of a make-up purse and I said 'Oh thank you.'

Then I suddenly realised that I hadn't bought anything for the little girl and I felt tight and stupid. What on earth was I thinking? The little girl was looking at me, all wide eyed, probably in anticipation of a gift and I hadn't thought to get her a little something. I hadn't even brought anything for Ritchie's parents! Whatever was I thinking! It had been so long since I'd spent Christmas with a real, happy-family but that was no excuse. It was inexcusable.

Whatever was I wearing? Ritchie's sister-in-law was all done up with a sparkly dress and so was the little girl. I was wearing jeans and an ordinary jumper! I felt such an out of place idiot! A bumbling fool. Ritchie was wearing jeans and a jumper too but he didn't look stupid at all, he didn't look out of place. This was his house, his parents house, he fitted in well. Not like me. Perhaps no one wanted me there really. Perhaps they were all pretending they did. Maybe they were all just going through the motions of being polite. I felt kind-of disconnected. An outsider. Disconnected from this family, disconnected from Christmas. Disconnected from everyone.

Being at other people's houses at Christmas was just so awkward and the memories of previous Christmases whizzed around through my mind. Childhood Christmases with Mum, dad, and sister. Christmas at my dad's house with his new wife and their child. The foster family. Lodging in Worcester, Christmas with Jimmy's family, Christmases alone, Mark and the twins, Andy, Kalvin! It was all whizzing around through my head light a washing machine.

Ritchie had already gone through, to chat to his parents, in the kitchen which led onto the dining room. Soon after our arrival, Ritchie's older brother arrived and then the whole family were all chatting in the kitchen while I sat in the living room alone. I knew I should make my way to the kitchen. I knew that I must join the festive chatter and cheer but I suddenly froze. I don't know what was really going on in my head but I couldn't do this. I felt like a fake, I felt I didn't belong, I was not one of them. I felt like a cuckoo.

I'd spent too many Christmases alone, I'd been hurt too many times, I was bereft for Worcester (although I was in denial of this,) and my own family, I was desperate for a little house on the prairie and here it was, the closest thing to it. Perhaps the closest thing I would ever have. I was in love with Ritchie and everything was good but something was wrong and I didn't know what! My head was in chaos.

I stood up and moved with the intention of making my way to the kitchen where enlivened chatter seemed to be getting increasingly elevated. Then I started to get really stressed. I couldn't face walking into the kitchen and everyone making a big Christmas fuss of me. It just felt wrong. I started to feel myself getting tearful and the more I tried to avoid my perplexing emotion the worse it got. I knew that in a few minutes someone would come and check on me and then they'd see me looking tearful and then I'd put a cloud on everyone's day. The confusion was increasing in intensity to the point where I was shaking and almost sobbing. I tried, in vain, to quickly analyse my perplexing thoughts, which only made things worse.

I felt I had no choice, I had to walk out of the house. I tiptoed out of the living room, opened the front door, stepped out and closed it as quietly as I could. As I hurried down the driveway, I cried with guilt at the thought of what I'd just done but I couldn't turn back. I looked an absolute mess.

I didn't know what to do for the best. I walked, as I cried, all the way back to the flat where I spent the rest of Christmas day alone. It's ironic isn't it. I had a chance to be part of a happy family for Christmas and I was no longer in a position to be able to cope with it!

I called Ritchie as soon as I got into the flat. I was so sorry and thought he'd be really angry about what I'd just done. But he was surprisingly chill. He was concerned about my mental health though and said he'd be with me within a couple of hours. It was embarrassing to think of my place being set at his family table and empty of me. How would I live it down and ever face his parents again?

The events of the festive season were soon forgotten and I felt comfortable again at the parents' house as long as it wasn't with the added pressure of Christmas. It's only as I look back that I realise how disturbed and fragile I really was.

I got along well with Ritchie's parents; his mother was a good seamstress and she lent me her spare sewing-machine with bit-by-bit instructions on how to master the craft of needlework. Although I'd shown a lot of potential for sewing, at school, it seemed I'd forgotten all I'd learned and now I wasn't very good at it, at all. But, having no daughters of her own, Ritchie's mum seemed happy that I was, at least, taking an interest in her favourite subject.

Ritchie was so laid-back that he was almost permanently horizontal when home, at the flat, with me. He still liked a drink, with his mates at the pub, and didn't intend to stop his regular outings. But he wasn't an alcoholic as two of my previous boyfriends had been. Weed was more his thing.

Ritchie's idea was, to move in with me and

continue as though he still lived at home with his parents. I would simply pick up where his mother had left off. But, where his mother had given him total freedom to come and go as he'd liked, I was so into him that I didn't want him out of my sight. If he went out and was later back than I'd anticipated, I'd get really stressed, really quickly. Then, on his return, I'd start going on at him.

With the benefit of hindsight, I think that I just wanted a lot of reassurance. I was afraid of the pain of grief if Ritchie were to leave me. The hurt I'd feel if he went with another girl. The fear I'd experience if he were to turn violent. The grief of being grief-stricken. And what if he backed his van into the driveway and took all my belongings. It could happen, I knew it could.

I was just so damaged and I suppose - mentally unwell - that I needed a lot of attention to confirm that we were still in love. But life is not so simple. And the more I demanded reassurance, the less I got it.

I made myself ill with worry when Ritchie was regularly late home. The more I worried, the crazier I appeared and consequently, the less interest he showed in me. Within a few months I'd taken the place of his mother as I continually picked up and cleaned up after him. He left his empty fizzy drinks cans everywhere. His shoes and other clothes were left where they dropped. His ashtrays were left full until I emptied them. And he was ever so slightly disrespectful towards me with his derogatory side-comments.

'Can you pick up all of your cans and put them in the bin?' I said, one night, with an aggressive tone.

'Nah, can't be arsed' Ritchie replied in his usual laid-back way.

That evening I got really frustrated with Ritchie, partly because of his nonchalant attitude and partly because I'd lost the plot. I was shouting and screaming at him about the mess he was leaving around all the time. But more than the irritation of his teenage behaviour, there was a difficulty of negotiating my general emotions around living with Ritchie. My past traumas were with me and I was fully triggered but I didn't even realise any of this at the time. Of course, he didn't understand, how would he when I didn't even understand myself. And even if he had understood, he wouldn't have put up with the way I was behaving. I felt threatened and rejected because I loved him so much and I had this mad energy like a terrifying earthquake within me. He didn't want to talk about anything, he just wanted to lay down with a spliff, while I did the hoovering. And I became very aggressive as I smashed the hoover into the wood of the bedframe. I wound myself up into a frenzy and was shouting hysterically and uncontrollably. The love I felt for him had made me mentally disturbed or maybe I had been for a while but this emotion had really lit the fire.

Suddenly, Ritchie stood up and put his shoes and jacket on. Then he said he was going out to get a Chinese takeaway. I tried desperately to calm myself down as he popped out. Around fifteen minutes later, the telephone rang. 'I'm not coming back Jen' Ritchie spoke. I immediately started freaking-out as my feelings of potential rejection got triggered again.

'No!' I screamed, 'you have to come ba..' Ritchie cut the call.

I kept calling him back on his mobile phone but he didn't answer and eventually his phoneline went dead.

I cried for a while. Then I tried to talk myself out of this panicky frenzy by telling myself that Ritchie would think the better of it and be home soon. But the words in my head wouldn't convince my physical symptoms. I'd gone into a state of trauma and the stress hormones were already racing through my veins. Ritchie didn't come back and I worried myself sick all night.

Next day I went to Ritchie's parents' house. As I arrived, Ritchie's lovely father made himself scarce by nervously sculking about in the back dining room. Meanwhile his mum sat me down, with a cup of tea in the living room and tried to calm me down. But she said she hadn't seen Ritchie at all. This seemed very odd as I felt sure he would have turned up at his parents' house by now. Now

I really was worried sick. If his parents hadn't seen him then where on earth was he! I was beside myself with worry.

That evening I went to the Charleston public house in tears, looking for Ritchie. One of his friends was there, he was so used to seeing me laughing and joking that he thought I was playing around when I came up to him, saying, 'Help me, please help me find Ritchie,' I was in such a state.

The days passed by like that and no one seemed to know where Ritchie was. Several times I turned up at his parents' house in floods of tears and his mum told me she also didn't know where he was. I suggested we should contact the police but Ritchie's mum considered that to be an unnecessary move. I could only assume all the worst-case scenarios. That he'd left me forever, that he was with another girl, that he was injured in a hospital or that he'd killed himself and was laying dead in a ditch somewhere!

After a week, I was more than hysterical! I went to Ritchie's mum and sat in her living room, I hadn't eaten or gone into my office job for days and I no longer worked at the pub. I was in a shocking state. His mum had made me a cup of tea and was again giving me her full attention in the living room. Then she suddenly turned her eyes in the direction of the front windows, then turned back abruptly to me saying, 'Ritchie's coming up the driveway.' I turned and looked and she was right! As he entered the house, she blocked him at the threshold to let him know that I was in the living room and he immediately turned around and left. I just looked at his mother in shock and horror.

'Don't go after him,' she said.

I'd already stood up ready to go, 'But I have to,' I insisted, 'otherwise I won't be able to find him again! I need to talk to him, I need to find out what's happening, I need to find out where he's staying!'

'He's come back home; he's been staying here,' She blurted out. 'I'm sorry, he didn't want you to know.'

'What. You mean, he's been staying here this whole week and you didn't tell me?'

'Yes, I'm sorry, I was sworn to secrecy.' She declared, 'He doesn't want to be with you anymore, he says you won't let him do anything, I think it's over'

I had no words left and just slowly walked out of the house.

I felt like someone had got a sharp knife and sliced me open from my throat and all the way down my breast-bone. I was cut open and the pain was excruciating. I could barely breath, the feeling of my heart breaking was so profound. On top of the grief of losing Ritchie, I'd been deceived by his mother. Her loyalty was, of course, to her son. But he really should have faced me and she should have made him man-up rather than covering for him and doing his dirty work.

Chapter 12

Stop

I was devasted again and could see no point in continuing life. Not just without Ritchie but the continuation of this circle of falling in love and the pain of grief. I couldn't eat at all so I purchased some cans of vitamin milk-drinks to try and prevent the faintness and sickness which had developed from a lack of sustenance. It would take me hours to get one can of the drink into me. I'd completely stopped eating and just took to my bed, hoping the misery would miraculously disappear. I just wanted the emotional pain to end but every time I awoke, no matter night or day, I'd immediately take a sudden sharp intake of breath as though I were drowning and trying not to go under the water. Then I'd just collapse on the bed in fits of tears and agony as I realised, I'd lost Ritchie and it was all my fault!

I became so weak and ill that I no longer had the strength to go into work at all. But I managed to get to the local doctor where I simply cried nonstop. The doctor gave me a one-month off-work certificate (signed off with clinical depression) and a prescription for a pack of antidepressants. I was also referred to a mental health counsellor while I waited for a clinical psychologist appointment.

Within a few days, Ritchie's parents drove around to my flat and gathered up Ritchie's belongings. This saved Ritchie the inconvenience and awkwardness of having to explain himself to me. His parents didn't stay long. But they stayed long enough for me to detect an abundance of sympathy in their eyes, especially when they had to ask for the leather jacket. Even though Ritchie had given it to me, as a present, he apparently wanted it back. I'd hurt him, harmed him - wasted his time and he was angry with me. He'd had high hopes of this relationship and I'd gone from a fun-loving eye-catcher to an insecure and unhinged mess. He was disappointed and angry that he'd gone to the trouble of moving his stuff in with me only to have to move it back out again. Up to this point, in his life, it was the most traumatic thing he'd been through and he was pissed off with me for it.

Ritchie's mother insisted I hold onto the sewing machine but I knew that without her teaching, I'd never learn how to sew. So, I insisted she take it, in the car, along with all the other stuff. We all said we'd keep in touch but we all knew that that was a big fat lie.

Nothing could be done to help the situation or

heal my pain. And even after Ritchie's belongings had been removed from the flat, I still thought he might come back to me. I suppose that's what you call pure Denial.

The initial counselling appointment came up quickly. The Counsellor was an older lady named Lillian. I didn't hold back and I told her everything on our first (and only) meeting. Everything that had hurt me over the years. I told her all about my relationships and especially my recent break-up with Ritchie. She listened and tried to write as much stuff down as she could. I told her everything, including embarrassing stories and things that I was ashamed of. When the hour was up, she checked the clock and said, 'Ok, time's up. Make another appointment, with the receptionist, for one day next week,' Then she covered her mouth, with her hand, in a jovial way and whispered, 'Then you can come back and tell me some more of your secrets!' She winked and I suddenly felt very exposed and wished I hadn't told her anything. I'd been too trusting in this official setting; I thought I was safe. But now I regretted telling her anything! I felt like an idiot. I felt even worse than before I went.

All my business would be written down now. I regretted going. I regretted opening myself up to this counsellor. I felt exposed and I immediately decided not to see Lillian again. I phoned the receptionist to let them know that I wouldn't be coming back for any further appointments but things are never so simple. The receptionist wanted to know why. It was difficult to explain without going through all of my personal business again. So, I started but then I stopped myself. Then I simply said I didn't think Lillian was a very good counsellor. The receptionist insisted she was very good, 'very experienced.' Check-mate, I gave up but I would not go there again.

Was I wrong to be angry that Lillian had joked about my hurtful life as my 'secrets.' Or had I overreacted and was I just too mentally unwell even for counselling? I never was sure about it and I'm still confused when I think of it because I stopped trusting my own instincts.

On occasion I would speak, on the phone, with Jaz or Suzie. They would try to encourage me out of my despair. But I passed most of the weeks alone with no one to talk to in the wreckage of a ship called Hope. The doctor wrote out another one-month certificate for me to remain off work and I passed my twenty-seventh birthday in a crisis. I was truly unfit for work.

'Hello, this is the Samaritans, my name is Daniel, I'm here to help you.' The sympathetic voice, on the other end of the telephone, spoke.

'I don't want to live anymore' I cried.

'Can you tell me what's lead you to this position?'

'Everything, just everything' I sobbed.

'Well, you mustn't do anything silly because, just think about your family and how upset they'd be'

'I don't have any family'

'Well, you still shouldn't harm yourself'

'Why not?

'Because you shouldn't'

'Ok thanks' Ever polite in all circumstances, I replaced the receiver and howled. Even the world-famous Samaritans couldn't help one bit. The guy really had no clue what to say and no words of any comfort. He seemed to be reading from a script. I would never call them again. I was really done with this life. I couldn't go on and remained in my bed without visitors and without real food.

Finally, after two months, I almost crawled into the British Telecom office. I'd lost over a stone and now weighed around seven stone which is around 44 kilograms. At the lower end of average height, I looked rather gaunt and painfully slim. Heads turned to look at me on my first day back, I was so weak and ill and in a wretched state.

I'd set myself a low-level challenge, for my first day back at work, to purchase a banana from the morning tea-trolly and somehow eat it. I sliced it into several pieces and placed one morsel into my mouth with a plastic fork. The chewing took forever and the swallowing was difficult. It must have been painful to watch but I doubt that anyone was watching. One piece an hour was about all I could manage. Meena sat with me during lunch-break and I just talked to her and cried. By the end of my first day back at work I'd managed to finish the browning banana.

That evening Suzie called to check if I was ok. I wasn't. And she suggested that she would come and visit me just before Christmas. She needed to do one of her trips out of Tunisia to get her passport stamped anyway. So, coming to me seemed like a sensible option at this point. Her idea was that me anticipating her arrival would give me something else to think about other than Ritchie. And it did help.

As the days passed, I slowly started being able to eat again, in the office canteen. I still felt heavily depressed but the weakness improved. My strength slowly returned until I started to, at least, be able to smile again.

Chapter 13

Positive

A black cloud lifted off of me as I started to recover from the breakup, which had happened in the early August before my twenty-seventh birthday in September. I had no recollection of that birthday at all. I may even have slept through it, under the influence of the doctor's medication.

Now it was the end of November and I was feeling a lot better. Not only had I weened myself off the antidepressants but I was back in my original position of Clerical Officer. I had been for a while now. Which meant I had more disposable income and I didn't need to worry about the lack of income from my finished part-time pub job. I continued with my application to purchase my flat under the 'Right to buy scheme.' If I manged to do this, it would give me more security and the legal right to rent it out, if I wanted to.

As my spirits lifted, I started taking driving lessons again and failed a second test. But this time I put in straightaway for a retake and finally I passed! That was something to be proud of at least.

Anyway, Suzie was planning on staying with me,

for a week, at the beginning of December and I was really looking forward to her coming. Since I was unhappy with living alone and my job and the repeated heartbreak, I was hoping that we could thrash-out some positive plans for my future life. Suzie cared about me and I knew that I could trust her with suggesting the best solutions for my future. I still felt sad when I thought about Ritchie and my previous pains. But in general, I was feeling stronger and a lot more positive. Just knowing that Suzie cared so much, helped to get me through. When someone's routing for you, praying for you, it helps a lot - I'm convinced of it.

December came around quickly. Suzie had managed to get herself on a chartered flight, with the holiday makers. So, she flew to Gatwick airport. I wanted to welcome her and help her with her luggage, so I took trains and buses across the city.

Suzie had a sister living in southeast London but she didn't want her to know that she was in town. They'd had their sibling rivalry and other issues in the past. I didn't really question it at the time. I was just glad to have her come to stay with me.

It was only on Suzie's stay with me that I noticed a scar poking out at the top out her shirt. It turned out that Susie had had a lot of health problems. She'd previously had open-heart surgery and had been sliced open through her breast-bone one time. It was radical surgery, which saved her life. She now had to take heart-medication every day for the rest of her life. She also took antidepressants and a whole bunch of other pills including sleeping tablets. She put in a request, at my local pharmacy, for her repeat list of medication. I picked it all up for her, as I passed by on my way home from work, on one of the days during her stay.

You never would have known that Suzie had so many serious health issues, by looking at her. She really looked after herself with personal grooming. She looked fantastic. Whilst staying with me she went to the hairdressers and got her blonde highlights redone. She bought herself high quality clothing. She had a regular skin-care routine with all the expensive products. She looked more like a forty-year-old than early sixties. She also wore expensive perfume which I guessed she got on her regular trips through duty-free. It was all good. She'd been through a lot, what with the messy divorce and the disappointing relationship with the young hotel-worker but now I guessed she was living the life out in Kerkennah. She was a trooper and I admired her.

'I have an idea!' Suzie announced, as I put our fresh cups of tea on the coffee table and sat down opposite her.

'Go on' I smiled.

'Well, since you're planning on buying this place,

you'll be able to legally rent it out to tenants.' She paused.

'Yeah, keep talking.' I said, as I wondered where she was going with this conversation.

'Well, I have a two-bedroom villa in Kerkennah and I know how unhappy you are here and how you love it there. You could rent-out this place and come and live with me, if you want to? You can stay as long as you want.' She looked at me in heightened anticipation of my response.

I had to pinch myself to be sure I wasn't dreaming! 'Oh wow! I'm not gonna even hesitate, yes, yes, wow, yes!' I felt overwhelmed in so many ways. To think that I could get out of this flat, yet still potentially own it. I could rent it out and yet always have it as a fall-back option (a little safety-net.) I could leave the monotony of my office job. I could live on the idyllic and tropical islands of Kerkennah. Perhaps I could even break this endless heartbreak cycle, if I had the constant company of a companion who cared about me. Heartbreak circle or self-harm circle, what difference, it was a cycle I was stuck in but maybe this was now my lucky break! Suzie and I would support each other and recover from our troubled lives - together.

Also, rumour had it that British Telecom were about to offer a voluntary redundancy package which in my case would mean a four thousand pound pay off! You could live for a couple of years without working, on that sum, in Kerkennah. But, best of all I had my substitute Mother who was asking me to come and live with her and stay as long as I wanted! After all of these years of feeling unwanted. This was just what I needed. A place to recuperate and recover in the sunshine with someone who really cared about me. And I could stay for as long as I wished!

'Thank you, I'll take the redundancy package and I'll come and stay with you! I'll do it!' I replied. I felt suddenly ecstatic.

We enjoyed the rest of our week together with walks in the park, hot soups and toast in the flat and a couple of trips to a local public house. It was all good and Suzie appreciated having a place to stay as she popped out of Tunisia for her visa-stamp trip. I knew I'd have to do those visa stamp trips soon but I was even looking forward to that too.

'Do you think you'll ever leave Kerkennah?' I said, as we made our way, by trains and busses, across London to Gatwick airport.

'No, I'll never live anywhere else.' Suzie said, as tears welled up in her eyes.

Suzie had suffered in life and I thought we understood one another. I saw her as an older version of myself and I suppose she saw herself in me. But I didn't understand why she got emotional that day. I guessed she had a lot of skeletons in her cupboards and was just struggling in life in general. Or perhaps she was just sorry to be saying goodbye to me on this day. She was probably worried and concerned about leaving me too, I'd been in such a bad state of late. But I'd be with her soon. Having me come to stay with her would be her tonic. We would lean on each other for emotional support and convince each other to be strong again, I felt sure we were both capable of recovering from life's beatings.

Anyhow, now Suzie was on her flight back to the islands where she would spend Christmas alone but at least she would be lonely in paradise. While I was stuck in the miserable and grey east end. But I could cope better now, knowing I had a plan of action. I would continue with my application for a mortgage on the flat which was now almost complete. And, since my company was offering voluntary redundancy, I would put in for it, take the money, rent out the flat to cover the mortgage payments and make my escape.

Unfortunately, it turned out that I wasn't entitled to the four-thousand-pound package redundancy deal because I'd had a break in my service to the company. Although I'd worked there for four years altogether, it only counted as two years because I'd left and re-joined, i.e., broken service. Therefore, I was only entitled to two-thousand pounds from the second half of my service. No matter, I planned on taking it.

Even two thousand could last a year in Kerkennah and cover the costs of my flights too. I didn't need much. I wasn't bothered about spending time and wasting money on nights out at the tourist zone. I just had visions of me and Suzie going on walks and sitting in the villa, watching the sunset on the balmy sea through the open windows.

I had to contact my uncle, by telephone, to arrange for my inheritance money to be transferred to my account as I needed it for the deposit on the flat. I'd hardly had any contact with him in years. He was still the trustee to my mother's will. My mother had expressly wished that this couple of thousand pounds only be inherited by my sister and I, as we each passed the age of thirty-five. Or before that, only as a deposit on a property or otherwise as the trustee considered necessary. I'd wanted to stick with my mother's plan of using it as a deposit on a property rather than receiving it at the age of thirty-five years with no plan. The bulk of it was saved for my deposit. I never asked for any of it prior to the day I requested it all for the deposit. Although my uncle had set up a regular small sum, which had gone into my account on a monthly basis. This was an amount of £25, since I'd been sixteen. My uncle had taken his position as trustee seriously and he'd invested my inheritance wisely. Therefore, the monthly £25 had been from the interest and the main amount was hardly touched and still available as a decent sized deposit.

Christmas passed and, in the January, the flat became legally mine with a mortgage.

I regularly spoke on the telephone with Suzie. It was easy enough to get hold of her by telephoning the Grand hotel. The receptionist, named Mahmood, would kindly get a message to Suzie as he lived in the same village as her. Then Suzie would get herself to the hotel and we'd chat for a while. She was always enthusiastic about me coming to stay with her. She'd listen with great interest as I relayed to her the latest situation with the flat and then the redundancy information. I'd discovered that the redundancy package would be available from the first of April, 'April fool's day in the UK,' and I would be the first with my hand up for it.

Chapter 14

Storm Clouds

There were several logistical issues, and hoops to jump through, on my way up to Easter. There were dealings with letting agents to find suitable tenants for my time away, which might well be forever. I was looking at a six-month rolling contract which I could continually extend, if need be. Then I needed to complete my redundancy application and pack up my personal belongings. I would pack all the stuff, which I couldn't take with me, into the small second bedroom of my flat and have a lock fitted on that door. The rest of the flat would be rentable without the second bedroom. I'd already packed most of my stuff up.

Then the day came for me to officially sign for the redundancy package. I did it and I spoke to Suzie that evening to let her know it was all done. She was very encouraging and seemed happy that I would be with her within a couple more weeks. I hadn't booked my flight yet but I was about to do it.

It was a Saturday afternoon as I looked out of the living room window, of the flat, and saw the storm clouds gathering. Black and grey clouds were circulating each other and squeezing together. I thought to myself how it didn't really matter anymore as I'd soon be back living in paradise, where the weather was always ideal.

There used to be an advertisement on television in the 1980s, 'In your dreams…you've… been to … Tunisia…' was the catchphrase. In the advert, a woman of approximately my age, swan in a crystal blue pool in the sunshine, there were palm trees and smiling faces all around her. I was miles away, in my mind, thinking about that advert, when the telephone started ringing and I got dragged back down to earth by the loud and constant sound.

'Hello' I said.

'Hello, is that Jenny?' A female voice asked.

'Yes,' I hesitated. I didn't recognise the voice at all.

'I'm a friend of Suzie, your friend Suzie, I'm very sorry to tell you that Suzie is dead…… hello, hello, are you still there?' This unknown woman questioned.

'What, what are you saying? How is this possible?'

'Well, you know Suzie was not a well woman don't you, she had a lot of health conditions.' She continued, 'I'm sorry but I thought you should know, I know you were planning to come out to Kerkennah and stay with her soon, so I thought I should let you know. I know she thought a lot of you.'

'I, I don't understand' I said.

'I'm so sorry, I know it must be a terrible shock.' She continued.

'Yes, but yes, it is, but...... thank you for letting me know.' I said as I replaced the receiver.

'This cannot be true,' I said to myself, it can't be!'

I lay down on my bed and stared up at the ceiling. 'No, it cannot be true, perhaps Suzie has changed her mind about me coming and got a friend to tell me this story to deter me?' But why? No, it can't be true, it just can't be.'

Then the telephone rang and startled me again. This time it was the voice of another woman, a crazy one. 'Is that Jenny? This is Suzie's sister. 'Would you like to tell me why Suzie came to stay with you in December and didn't even let me know that she was in London?' I'm her sister! Why? Why didn't she come and stay with me or even let me know she was in London?!!' She demanded.

I was stunned into silence; I was just so shocked. Was Suzie really dead? Was this really her sister? 'You better tell me now! Why was Suzie with you? Interpol are involved, so you better tell me everything you know right now or they'll be coming to interrogate you,' she continued, she was in an absolutely hysterical and distraught state.

'What does Interpol mean?' I asked, as I felt myself starting to shake uncontrollably.

'The International Police!' She shouted, 'Suzie may have been murdered, there's blood splattered up the walls, everywhere!'

'Oh no' I managed to reply as I started to break down.

'You'll have to tell Interpol why she came to you and not me' She continued. And with that she put the telephone down.

I lay on my bed and stared up at the ceiling, in a state of shock. 'No, no, no it can't be true, Suzie's dead? She's been murdered? How and why?!

I got up and telephoned Jaz but she was out, so I told Jaz's mum that two women had called me and told me that Suzie was dead. One had implied that she'd died of natural causes and the other one had insinuated that she'd been murdered. Of course, Jaz's mum didn't know what to say so she just said that she'd let Jaz know when she got back in.

I didn't get undressed that evening, I just lay on my bed, fully dressed, all night with the light on, staring up at the ceiling saying, 'No surely not, it can't be true, she can't be dead, no, no, no'

I didn't sleep all night. In the morning I called the hotel Grand. There were some kind and decent people working there as well as the dodgy ones. Mahmood recognised my voice and he immediately broke down and I knew right away that it was true, Suzie was gone.

'What happened to Suzie?' I asked tentatively.

'She die' He cried.

'Yes, I know but how and why?' I asked, gently.

'She kill herself!' He replied. 'She take barsha medicament in one and she die'

Being the hotel receptionist, Mahmood normally spoke in almost perfect English. But he was clearly distraught and was now speaking in his native Arabic mixed with French and almost unintelligible broken English.

'Barsha medicament? Oh, that means a lot of medicine or too much medicine?' I questioned.

'Yes, Barsha' He explained.

Now there were three possibilities - that Suzie had died from her ailments, that she'd been murdered or that she'd taken her own life.

To break the silence in my flat, I had the radio on for some company. When this tune played.

'And the storm clouds gather overhead'

'No shelter we can share'

'Lay down on my flower bed'

'I got no control'

'I would sell my soul'

'To be there'

And finally, the first tears rolled down my face and

I started to believe it was true. Suzie was gone. But still I went in and out of believing and disbelief. And then numbness again.

I don't know why I was so terrified about Interpol contacting me but in the end they never did. I guess they had enough information without my input. I guess they were satisfied with the evidence at hand - about the cause of death. But I never did discover the whole truth about Suzie's departure from this world. Her friend had suggested that Suzie had died of natural causes. It was true that she was not a well woman. Then her sister had suggested that she'd been murdered. She said that there'd been blood splatted up the walls! But she was clearly hysterical on hearing of the death. And angry because Suzie had chosen to stay with me for her last trip to England. I'd been thrown into shock and was not forthcoming with her quest for information. Perhaps she'd said there was 'blood up the walls,' to shake me up and make me explain Suzie's actions. But I felt loyalty to Suzie and couldn't divulge what she'd told me about her relationship with her sister. Suzie hadn't told me much anyway. She'd only said that she'd prefer to come to me rather than her sister. But she'd told me this in private and I wouldn't break her confidence dead or not dead. At the time I couldn't believe she was dead anyway. And I didn't want to hurt Susie's sister by telling her that Suzie had preferred to spend her last trip to England with me rather than her!

I would never know for sure but I think Mahmood was right. I think Suzie took the cocktail of pills that I'd picked up for her from my local pharmacy, when she'd stayed with me. She was not a well woman or a particularly happy one. Heart pills combined with antidepressants and sleeping tablets would have been more than enough to terminate her slim frame, to end her life. But why had she encouraged me to rent out my flat and take redundancy from my job? Why had she come up with the idea that I should recuperate with her in Kerkennah, in the first place!? And why had she committed suicide just two weeks before I was planning on going there?

I would never know. I would never comprehend why Suzie had taken these actions. She must not have been in her right mind at all. Our whole relationship had been based on her mothering me when all the time she'd needed to be mothered! I felt awful to think of the dreadful state she must have been in during her last days, hours, minutes, and seconds. During our friendship it had always been me who'd talked of ending it all while she'd always listened and persuaded me out of it. Damn it, I only called the Samaritans because Suzie had suggested it! And now I know why she'd suggested it. She knew I was suicidal because suicide was in the forefront of her own mind and all that time she was thinking of ending herself!

Chapter 15

What now

I guess I was still in a state of shock when I went into work on the Monday morning. Meena was in a chirpy mood as she bounced over. 'Hey you've only got till next Friday and then you're off, lucky you!' She spoke and then as she noticed my demeanour, 'hey what's up?'

'Suzie died' I said, then I continued by explaining everything of what I knew from the weekend.

'Oh my God, what're you gonna do? You'll have to try and cancel your redundancy if they'll let ya' Meena continued.

'Yeah, I don't know, I just don't know'

Over the next few days, I stayed like that, in and out of a state of numbness. Even now, when I think of Suzie, I struggle to believe she's not still there, living in the villa, overlooking the balmy sea, in Kerkennah. I don't know what happened to her body. If she was buried there or if she was flown back to England. I didn't have contact numbers for the woman who'd called me initially, to let me know Suzie was dead. I didn't have Suzie's sister's number either. Anyway, at this point, I didn't want to think about it. I probably wouldn't have got a straight answer out of anyone anyway. I didn't know who to believe. But I had to decide what I would do next. Suzie's idea of me staying with her for a peaceful recovery and recuperation, was suddenly curtailed. She'd abruptly ended it all and Kerkennah was out of the question now.

The letting agency rang me. They'd found a couple of young professional men who were keen to rent my flat at the agreed price. They'd been vetted and their deposit had already been taken. I told the agency that I needed a few days before I would sign anything. I told the agent that if I were to let the flat, I would also require their property management service as I had no one else to help me with picking up the rent et cetera.

A few days passed and still I was in and out of numbness. Maybe I could just cancel the redundancy application and remain in the flat. Maybe I could stay working at British Telecom. I could probably go back and work at the Charleston again at weekends and evenings. Or I could work at another public house. I would probably recover from the loss of Suzie, in time. I could forget about Kerkennah, forget about Tunisia. Another guy would come along for me soon enough, I surmised. I looked at myself in the mirror, I hardly recognised myself, I was dead behind the eyes.

No! I couldn't face it. I couldn't continue this

life of a rotten roller-coaster ride. The boredom of my office-job, the excitement of new love and the misery of heart-break and loneliness. I needed people in my life, people who cared about me like my substitute mother did. I could barely live with the bereavement of Suzie and the disappointment of my dreams of the tropical recuperation being ended. I had to still make it happen! I had to get out of this concrete jungle. But how?

I decided I would continue with my plans as if nothing untoward had happened. I signed the agreement with the letting agency for the two professional guys to rent my flat. And the agency took their fee from the deposit, which they'd already taken. I continued packing my belongings into the second bedroom. I let my redundancy application tick along.

I bought a one week package-holiday to the mainland city of Sousse in Tunisia, with the intention of overstaying. Perhaps, in a big city like Sousse, I could find employment as a holiday representative and make a life for myself there. Sure, it wasn't with Suzie and it wasn't the same as Kerkennah. But it was still in the foreign land that I'd fallen in love with. It was tropical and with a holiday atmosphere where I could socialise. I'd found it easy to make new friends in Kerkennah - Tunisia and just about impossible in Forest Gate - London, England. There were no jobs for me on the islands but on the mainland, I was in with a chance.

The final Friday came and it was my last working day at British Telecom. I took the lift to the top floor and said goodbye to the kitchen girls and continued my way down through each and every floor of the building to bid farewell to everyone, individually. I was like that. I thought that everyone deserved a minute or two of my time and effort - whether they wanted it or not was another thing. I would never see the majority of them ever again and I thought that working together had meant something. To me it had anyway. I started on the top floor and worked my way down to the first floor, (the ground floor held no real offices these days, only the security team, storage, and the elevator.)

The majority of my colleagues claimed to be envious of my escape from British telecom. Saying things like, 'Lucky you' and 'Oh I'm so jealous,' and 'Oh I wish I had the balls to just up and leave.' The last person I spoke to was Kalvin. He looked shocked when I held my hand out to shakes his.

'I just wanted to say goodbye and good luck with everything' I said.

'Erm, Yeah, I heard you were leaving, erm, where're you going? He spoke.

'Tunisia,' I said, with an unassured half-smile on my face.

'Tunisia!' He replied, with a half-frown and a confused look, 'Is that a job?!'

'Yeah, Bye.' I let go of his hand, I turned from him and walked towards the office door.

From behind myself, I heard his voice say a slightly stunned, 'Bye,' but I didn't look back.

I smiled and waved goodbye to the security team and left my photo-identification card on the front desk of the ground floor. The glass-doors slid open and I was free. But freedom is overrated. The freedom I had, meant running away from everything. This neck of the forest meant little to me anyway. So, I would leave it, run away, and recreate myself. I was starting all over again. Like that, perhaps everything would fall miraculously into place. But you can't run away from yourself can you.

I felt so isolated and lonesome. I felt that no one could or would help. Boyfriends had been coming and going and leaving me in a worse state. Friends were few and far away and I felt disconnected from them anyway. Professional counsellors and therapists didn't seem to understand me at all.

I'd recently been on a waiting list for a clinical psychotherapist referral. I'd finally got the appointment block and gone along with hopes to be cured of my afflictions. It was a strange experience. At our first meeting the male therapist hadn't spoken at all and waited for me to speak.

I had a lot of issues and stories to tell so, after an awkward silence, I bit the bullet and spilled. Things which I thought might be relevant to my current unhappy state. Past depression, repeated mistakes etcetera. He would close his eyes and sometimes, I thought he was sleeping. When I mentioned that I thought his behaviour to be rather odd, it was put back onto me. 'I wonder why it bothers you? He spoke.

I had a plethora of psychological problems, including bereavement, relationship issues, panic disorder, nightmares, extreme emotional responses etcetera. I had plenty of places, in my history, where this could have all originated from. I had plenty of material to deal with, from a psychological point of view. With hindsight, I don't think the therapist knew where to start with me and just opted for my 'unresolved issues with my father' and forced me to talk about it over and over. It was torturous and unhelpful.

When the therapist started missing appointments I got really frustrated and he put it back onto me, 'I wonder why it bothers you so.' I gave up with him. My only regret was that I didn't give up sooner than I did. I shudder when I think back on those appointments.

Things hadn't worked out with Lillian the counsellor either and even the Samaritans had failed to help. There was just no one and I'd been through rivers of tears, alone.

Thought is internalised dialogue and I was spending way too much time in dialogue with myself, that is, me and my thoughts. In a healthy life, we should have caring people around us to whom we can express our thoughts and concerns, laughter, and tears. It shouldn't be down to paid professionals. When money comes into the equation, we never really know if they care or if what they're saying, in a professional capacity, is true or they're just keeping you on their books to keep the cash rolling in. Ideally, we should be nestled in a sequence of hierarchical relationships, grandparents, parents, siblings etc. In conversations with our loved ones, they react to our words and we react to theirs. In an ideal scenario we should be able to thrash-out our concerns in a safe and trusted environment and reach conclusions. That is to take counsel from those we trust, our loved ones! No one should be expected to navigate this world alone. Insanity waits there.

The narrative through which I saw the world, was completely fractured. And because of that, my perceptions and emotional responses had often become chaotic - often producing a chronic stress response. I suppose I was subconsciously trying to nestle myself into something. I was driven to be in the comfort of a man's arms and in the company of others. I enjoyed conversation and would often babble on to random strangers with little encouragement. I was keen to be surrounded and submerged in love and I knew I wouldn't find it here, in England. It stood to reason as I'd failed so many times previously. So, I took a gamble - out of the continent of Europe and into North Africa.

Chapter 16

Sousse

My work colleagues had believed me to have 'balls' to up and leave and travel to North Africa - alone. But I knew it was desperation, rather than confidence, which had led me to this continent.

I was in the hotel Salem in the centre of the bustling city of Sousse. A highly touristic place, in a country which relied upon tourism for the majority of its income. The main strip was several miles in length with hotel after hotel stealing the beautiful sandy beachfront. The sky was a perfect blue and the air had a fragrance of jasmine, fried fish, and suntan lotion.

I didn't have much of a plan. Only to stay in the hotel Salem for a week whilst asking staff-members for help on where to rent accommodation for myself. After achieving that first step, I would search for work as a Holiday Representative or something else if that were not possible. Anything to prevent me from being back in that concrete box, being repeatedly in emotional pain, back in lonely town.

My mortgage payments would be covered by my

tenants back in London and I had access to two thousand pounds in my bank account. But Sousse turned out to be a much more expensive place than Kerkennah, so finding work would really be an urgent necessity, if I were to stay for any length of time as intended.

Seven nights stay with breakfast, was included in my original package. By the sixth night I still hadn't made any arrangements for accommodation and I was getting worried and irritable. I'd spoken to several members of staff in my quest for something suitable but thus far nothing had come from those conversations. It was like they weren't taking me seriously when I told them I would not be taking my return flight to England. I guess they'd heard it all before and I suppose they had better things to concern themselves with. It was my life, my problem and why should they care.

Then it came to the end of the week and my breakfast-waiter promised me that he would take me to a flat somewhere slightly inland from the main strip. I sat and waved goodbye to the holiday-makers on the coach that I should have been on, it was bound for the airport. I sat, in the sunshine, on a little wall with my travel bags. There I waited for the young waiter to meet me at the front of the hotel, as he finished his breakfast shift.

The waiter came and we took a taxi together. But instead of taking me directly to the flat, which I hoped to rent, he took me to meet his mother in the flat where he lived. I guessed he was just being hospitable. I had little understanding of what was going on. I had a poor comprehension of the mixed French and Arabic language which they spoke and I really struggled to make myself understood. But the waiter was able to translate into English somewhat.

The waiter's mother was really smiley and friendly. She kept putting different items in front of me for my consumption. Tunisian bread, dates, cakes, black-olives, water, a very sweet mint tea, Fanta orange and coffee. It was all very hospitable but I just wanted to get to the accommodation. I needed to get myself sorted. I didn't mean to be rude but I just wanted to get out of there.

The waiter was crudely translating between his mother and I. It was all a little awkward but I just kept smiling, until my jaw hurt. Then the waiter translated that his mother had asked if I would marry her son and I'd laughed and said 'No, bien sur no' (No, of course not, - in poor French.) I thought she was joking! I didn't mean to offend anyone. I just didn't know what was going on here and I wanted to get to my new accommodation. But I had offended her, it was obvious by the look on her face. Her voice became raised and fiery and the waiter stopped translating.

Shortly after this faux pas, the waiter removed me from his mother's home and took me to a block of flats called Zowie Moble, which means Zowie Furnished, as in furnished apartments named Zowie. It was a big echoing building, purpose built as one and two bedroomed, self-contained, furnished flats. Several streets back from the beach strip. I was taken to the office on the ground floor where the waiter spoke Arabic to the office guy and explained my situation before making a quick exit.

I then paid an equivalent to six hundred pounds for two months' rent up-front and was shown to my accommodation which was on the second floor of the four-storey building. The studio apartment consisted of a small living room/bedroom with two single beds, a small kitchen and a small shower room. I can't say that there was anything wrong with the flat which was clean, tidy and basic. But I just felt so incredibly lost. I felt homesick but I didn't know where I was homesick for, it certainly wasn't for my east London flat. Perhaps for my home city of Worcester and the Malvern hills but I couldn't even admit to that because there was nowhere to go there, no roof there - for my head.

'What have I done,' I said to myself as I sat all alone. 'What am I doing here?' The fear and the solitude were intense. I could hear a lot of activity, strange sounds and Arabic shouty, voices.

I didn't want to unpack that night; I didn't want to stay there at all but I didn't want to go back to England either. And even if I did, my London flat was now legally rented out to others. I had nowhere else to go there, so I had to make this situation work out, somehow.

Eventually, I fell into a strange half-sleep and was jolted awake by a nearby call to prayer from a local mosque. And seconds later another muezzin called out from another local minaret. Because I didn't understand any of the words at that time, it made me nervous. But eventually I was so exhausted that it lulled me into an altered state of consciousness and then a deep sleep.

Next day I popped down to the Zowie office and managed to get some information on the local area. Then I made my way out and found a post office. I sent a post-card to the letting agents (in London) to let them know my new Tunisian address. All of my post could be forwarded to me there, as part of their property management services. Then I made my way to a supermarket called the Mono-Prix and purchased a few essential items for my new place in Zowie Moble. Bread, butter, milk, croissants, coffee and shower-gel.

'Aslema Guida' A young man called out to me, as I came out of the supermarket with my shopping.

Well, I knew that 'Aslema' meant 'Hello' but I wasn't sure about 'Guida' so I didn't reply. But then I thought about it and realised that 'Guida' meant guide as in tour-guide, as in holiday representative. Because I was walking alone (most holiday makers were afraid to walk alone in Tunisia) and because I was carrying bags of shopping, I didn't look like a holiday maker and it was assumed that I was a new guide.

I took the bags of shopping back to the Zowie apartment, took a quick shower and made myself a coffee, along with a buttered croissant. Then I changed clothes and made my way back out to the main strip. My intention was to locate the local offices of the English touristic companies of which I'd discovered there were currently only two. I needed to become a holiday representative/guide; I didn't think there was any other job I could do. And I needed a job tout-suite.

'Aslema Guida' another male voice called out to me.

'Aslema' I replied, 'Do you speak English?'

'Yes, of course, a little,'

'Do you know where the Cosmos office is please'

'You guida?'

'Erm no'

'You have Tunisian boyfriend?'

'No, do you know where the Cosmos office is!?'

'Yes, you go direct here then left here, you meet me for coffee tonight?'

Oh dear, I just wanted directions and this guy was hitting on me. But I managed to get away from him and I managed to find the Cosmos office.

It was a relief to hear the chatter of the English women as I entered the office. They were extremely friendly towards me until they realised that I wasn't one of their clients. I was just another English woman looking to become a Holiday Rep.

'You have to apply in the UK, we don't recruit here,' One of the women said, in a rather abrupt manner.

'Oh, oh, oh I see,' I stuttered, 'Can you give directions for me to get to the Panorama offices?'

'Sure, it's directly opposite the Mono-Prix,' she said, 'I take it you have a Tunisian boyfriend?'

'No, no I don't.' I replied as I left the office.

'Well, you will have soon.' She called out after me. 'Every tourist woman gets one, hahaha'

I left the Cosmos office with a flea in my ear and headed back in the direction of the main Supermarket. All hopes were now pinned on working with this one company called - Panorama.

'Aslema,' more male voices called out, as I made my way back to the main strip.

Another young man blocked my path, 'You live Zowie Moble' he said. I was unsure if this was a question or he was just stating a matter of fact.

'Yes, I do live there, how do you know that? I

replied with a smile on my face.

'I see you, everybody see you.'

I dropped my smile and quickly made my way in the direction of the Mono-Prix, then I crossed the road and located the Panorama Agency.

A blonde woman sat alone behind a large, clumsy-wooden desk there and greeted me as I entered her office. She was easily fifteen years older than myself. She was friendly, her name badge read, 'Panorama, Head Rep - Yetta.' She had an unusual accent and I couldn't place it. She was chatty and happy to tell me about her situation. I got the feeling she felt bored sitting there all day, by herself, in this small airconditioned office.

Her name was Yetta, she was Danish, happily married to a nice local man and she had two teenage children. 'What's your situation?' She asked. Her English was excellent and I guessed that was one of the reasons why she'd managed to land the job of Head Rep, with an English company!

'Well, I'm living at Zowie Moble and I'm looking for work as a Rep.' I said with fake confidence.

'Do you have a Tunisian boyfriend?' She asked.

'No, I don't.' I replied with slight irritation. 'Why does everyone keep asking me that?'

'Because if you don't have a boyfriend, you'll be hounded by all the local men until you do have one.' Yetta explained. 'It's just a cultural thing and they don't mean any harm by it.'

'Yeah, I spent a couple of months on the islands of Kerkennah but I didn't notice it so much there,' I replied. I suppose I'd always been with Jaz there and I was known to be with Ahmed. That made sense, the others would back off once you were seen as 'taken.' I was starting to understand the rules now.

'Yes, I know Kerkennah well,' Yetta announced. 'We have the Hotel Grand there.'

I proceeded to tell Yetta about my friend Suzie who'd lived on the island but before I could tell the whole story Yetta butted in.

'She committed suicide,' Yetta said, rather abruptly, 'so you were the girl who was planning on moving in with her?'

'Yes, I was, I was all ready to go and then I heard the terrible news.' I spoke. I was amazed how news travelled so fast around in this country.

'By the way, we don't have any availability for new reps, the summer season is just underway and all the places are taken. You normally should apply in England you know, but I'll keep you on the books just in case something turns up,' Yetta smiled with only the bottom half of her face, which meant she was just going through the motions of being polite. We both knew that I had next to no chance.

'Yes, I know, are there any other tourist companies I could try out for or is there any other work I could do here in Sousse?' I asked with sudden desperation in my tone.

'No, there's only Panorama and Cosmos at the moment. Owners Abroad will start next year, maybe, but they're not here yet. There's nothing else you can work as here; you can't legally work anywhere else as you'll need a Carte de Sejour/a residence permit and you can't work without it. You have no right to stay in Tunisia for more than three months as a tourist you know. I wish you good luck.'

Back at Zowie I contemplated my existence and my reasons for coming to Tunisia. I'd already paid out for two months' rent and I could legally stay in the country for up to three months. So, I decided to try and make the most of my situation. Worst case scenario - I'd simply have an extended vacation which isn't much fun when your life is all upside down. But anyway, I would hang out at the nearest hotel to my accommodation and hope for the best, then I'd fly back to England and who knows what I'd do there in that God-forsaken place.

Chapter 17

Marhaba

Marhaba means 'Welcome' in Arabic. The Marhaba hotel was a beautiful four-star welcoming establishment. And just because I was obviously European, I was allowed to frequent the bars and the swimming pools, for free, as often as I pleased. While the local Tunisians were only allowed in as workers or if they were known to be rich or if they had friends in high places.

I started to regularly make my way to the hotel Marhaba and week on week I got to know the different holiday makers as they came and went. People were happy and in a holiday mood and a lot of them seemed keen to talk with me. They seemed to find my situation interesting. They were mostly friendly towards me and in some bizarre way, I felt I had some purpose in being there. I didn't know much yet, about the area of Sousse or Tunisian culture, but I knew more than they did and I felt of some use as I could answer some of their questions. And week on week my knowledge increased.

Most of the clients, in this hotel, were English

while a smaller proportion were Dutch. One evening I was sitting alone in the hotel bar when a Dutch guy approached me. 'My friend, over there, would like you to go out with him to the Marhaba club,' He explained with a strong Dutch accent.

'Where's your friend?' I said, as I looked around.

'Over there.' He spoke. 'The one with dark red hair, they call him Rouge, this is French word for red.'

At that moment my eyes caught with Rouge's eyes and the biggest smile broke across his handsome face. His smile was contagious and I was compelled to smile back.

'Is he Dutch?' I asked.

'No, he is not Dutch.' The Dutch guy explained.

'Well, he doesn't look English so, if they call him Rouge, I guess he's French then?' I spoke.

'So, you agree to go across to the club with Rouge? Marhaba club is right next door.' He replied. He was clearly a man focused on a mission and he was yet to answer my question about Rouge's nationality.

Rouge had an entrancing smile and I was easily distracted by it. I found I couldn't even hesitate. It was like I was under his spell or something. 'Yes, I'll go to the club with Rouge.'

The Dutch guy introduced Rouge and I to each other, then he made up his reasons to excuse himself from our company. Rouge spoke English very well, albeit with a strange accent which definitely wasn't French. We made our way over to the Marhaba club where Rouge spoke to the entrance staff in, what seemed to me to be, fluent Arabic!

'You speak Arabic?' I said, in surprise, I was impressed.

'Yes,' An extremely proud expression came over his charming face. 'I am Tunisian.'

'What, really!?' I questioned in disbelief.

'Yes, you don't believe me?' He asked.

'Well you just look so, I don't know, it's unusual, isn't it, to see a Tunisian with red hair?' I was gobsmacked.

'I have two brothers who are red like me and twin sisters who're brown' He explained.

'Wow.' I said, 'Well that's a first, I thought you were Dutch or French!'

'No, I am a Tunisian man with a silver shop.' He said, with a great deal of pride.

So, here he was, everyone said I had to have one and here, I'd found him, my Tunisian boyfriend. I was totally smitten.

As soon as a girl was seen out with a guy, in Sousse, they were automatically known as 'a couple.' If a girl was seen out with one guy on one occasion and then seen with another on another occasion, bad things would be said about her character. She would be considered lose. This may not have been a problem for female holiday-makers who were in and out of the country within a couple of weeks with no concern for their own reputations. But for Reps and anyone staying longer, they needed to watch how they behaved. It may have seemed 'old fashioned' by European standards but a girl's reputation was everything in Tunisia. Luckily for me, I was happy with the assumption that Rouge and I were a couple as, as far as I was concerned, we were - right from the offset.

At first I thought that Rouge owned the antique silver shop in the medina, in the heart of the souk. I don't know where I got that impression from. But anyway, it turned out that he didn't own it, he just worked there. But I didn't mind, I wasn't the silver or gold-digger type. To me, love was everything. This was the case for most single English women who found themselves in this dry and arid land of hope and paradise.

Most female tourists were afraid to go to the medina, as they'd heard that the local men would hassle them there. But it turned out that there was really nothing to fear. The guys would look but they'd never touch and, in some ways, I realised that I was safer there than in London. But female holiday makers rarely ventured outside of their hotels alone. The staring scared them and put them off. They always stuck in twos, at least, if they did go out at all. Ironically, couples drew more attention to themselves like this. Their conversation could be overheard and it was obvious which country they came from and that they were holiday-makers. They were a clearer target, yet they had a false sense of security and felt safety in huddling up in couples and groups. I had never ventured out alone in Kerkennah, for the same reasons of this false sense of security. But in Sousse, I was independent. And because I appeared confident, while walking alone, I was assumed to be either a guide or in a relationship with a local. Both of these assumptions put me in a more respectable position. I got used to the staring, it was really nothing to worry about. I was becoming comfortable in Sousse and I really wanted to stay.

Sometimes I would still be approached my men on the street but my learned reply would usually keep the conversations to a minimum. 'Aslema Guida' was the most common conversation tester with me. I would confidently reply 'Aslema' (without the encouragement of smiling!) and that would usually be the end of it. On occasion I'd be asked if I was 'married with Tunisian' and I would be honest in my reply which would, unbeknown to me, then put me in a more vulnerable position. Asked if I had a Tunisian boyfriend, up until this point, I'd answered 'no' in honesty but I soon realised why the other Reps had said that I had to have a Tunisian boyfriend. Otherwise, the men just wouldn't leave me alone. Anyway, by now I did have a boyfriend, so I no longer needed to worry and I could be honest in my reply. Yes, I did have a Tunisian boyfriend.

I enjoyed being out on my own in the medina and souk. I smiled to myself when the locals would suggest I'd been Tunisian in a previous life, I felt at home there. Even the sound of the mosque didn't make me nervous anymore, I found it soothing. I loved the smell of the spices, local food, the culture, the music, the people, and I made effort to learn their language which they in turn appreciated.

The hierarchy of respect towards European females went like this,

1 European woman married to a Tunisian man = highly respected.

2 European woman with one Tunisian boyfriend = well respected.

3 Guide/Holiday Representative/Rep = automatically respected.

4 European woman married to European man = hardly respected.

5 European woman with European boyfriend = disrespected.

6 European woman seen only in the company of other females = usually disrespected.

7 European woman seen in the company of more than one man on two separate occasions = highly disrespected.

But trumping all of these levels, if a European woman converted to Islam, she would be highly respected, celebrated and held up high as an example to others. Converting was not an easy thing to do and the locals rightly appreciated that.

This hierarchy took time to decipher and understand and as you can see, it was easy to innocently fall into the lower ranks of respectability without even realising.

One day I was trying to get across the busy main-road on my way to the Medina. I'd been attempting to cross there for ages but the drivers were erratic and I was starting to give up hope of crossing without getting injured. Then I saw a policeman so, in broken French and Arabic, I asked for help across the road. And no sooner had I asked for his assistance.

'Are you married?' he questioned without hesitation.

'Oh my God' I muttered under my breath and then in my best broken French I said, 'Yes, yes I am married - with Tunisian.' And that was the end of that conversation, he held up his hand and two cars immediately screeched to a halt to allow me to cross. From now on I would always say 'I'm married with Tunisian' at the beginning of all conversation with local men. It was the only way forward.

Chapter 18

Guida

I'd been living at Zowie for almost two months now. I'd spent my time hanging out at the hotels with holiday-makers. I'd mooch about in the Medina and visited Rouge in the souk. But I knew I couldn't continue for much longer like that.

I didn't like living alone in the apartment (any more than I liked living alone in Forest Gate) but at least I had a boyfriend here. I had places to go to socialise and faces that recognised me and seemed pleased to know me. And fabulous weather of course. But I didn't know quite what to do next.

Rouge visited me at Zowie but he never stayed over. It would be disrespectful to his parents he'd said. And it looked like I could never get a job as a Holiday Representative, I would never have an income or a residence permit or appropriate health insurance. Like that I had no legal right to remain in the country for more than three months at a time, so I had to consider what I would do next.

With hindsight, I really should have taken out medical insurance. It had been automatically included in the two-week package holiday to Kerkennah and my first week (package) at the hotel Salem. Jaz and I had been lucky during our two months stay in Kerkennah (without insurance) and I just hadn't even thought of the possible consequences of not having it.

Rouge had this proud yet charming character and a power over me. I guess he'd had plenty of experience with European women and girls and knew all of my weak spots, before I even met him. But then again, all of the locals had us sussed-out, because tourism had been the main business of Sousse for two generations and it was what they all knew. But we didn't appreciate the hidden agendas and many women were like lambs to the slaughter there.

I was never sure if it was just a cultural thing or if Rouge just wasn't all that into me. Since I'd made it clear that I was crazy about him, he seemed to turn up late for our dates and on occasion he didn't turn up at all. This upset me but I'd put it behind me on our next date and still we were together. I put his nonchalance down to cultural issues. He was a man who needed to be in control. And perhaps he needed to protect himself from emotional involvement as I could be gone within weeks or days. So, I couldn't blame him for that.

It was June and peak holiday season and I was walking down the main-strip near to the Mono-Prix supermarket. It was incredibly hot. I was thinking about leaving the Zowie apartment as the two months were nearly up and I didn't really want to continue my stay there. But what other options did I have? I could pay for an expensive stay, in a hotel, for a month, maybe I'd feel happier there. Then maybe I'd give up and return to England as my three-month automatic visa would be up. But I still wanted to stay in Tunisia and I wanted to be with Rouge. And anyway, where would I go in England and what would I do there?

'Jenny, Jenny, wait, Jenny!' Who was this European woman huffing and puffing and running after me! It was Yetta, the Danish woman from the Panorama office. 'Jenny, wait, let me get my breath back, oh it's so hot, I've been looking for you, I thought I would have bumped into you before now, do you still want to be a Rep? We had a Transfer Rep come over a couple of weeks ago, she stayed for a week, she hated it here and went back to England, if you want the job, please come to the office with me right now.'

'Yes, of course I do, come on let's do it!' I said, with the biggest smile.

I sat in the office with Yetta and we completed the paperwork together. I was now suddenly employed by the English travel company - Panorama! And as such, I was intitled to a Carte de Sejour/residence permit, company health insurance, a small monthly wage and reimbursement of my future taxi fares. But best of all, I was entitled to a room in the Guide house for free! I couldn't believe my luck. I was overcome with joy. I immediately left the Zowie apartment and took a taxi to the house. I took a receipt from the taxi driver under Yetta's say-so, I would be reimbursed later.

Rouge also seemed happy that I was now able to stay in the country. He knew about the Guide house and said it was not far from his home, which was slightly inland. But the guide house was overlooking the beach! I was so thrilled about my new job, accommodation, and my right to residency that Rouge couldn't help getting excited with me. Perhaps now he would allow his feelings to get involved with mine.

Most of the Guides, in the guide house were Danish, who worked for their travel company called Tjaereborg. Five of them lived upstairs while only two of us English were downstairs on the ground floor. Downstairs also accommodated the Tjaereborg offices.

I met my colleague and housemate, Denise. She'd been a fully qualified nurse in England but now she was one of Panorama's Hotel Reps. She was a lovely girl and we got alone fine. There were other Hotel, Transfer and Children's Reps too but the other Sousse ones lived with their Tunisian husbands. Only Denise and I were unmarried although we both had a Tunisian boyfriend each, of course. And guess where Denise came from? Malvern in

Worcestershire! We became best of friends and overtime my Worcester accent popped back up on occasion. How strange is that, that my Worcester accent made a temporary return to me in Tunisia, of all places!

It's strange the things you miss when you live overseas. Due to Denise's accent constantly reminding me, I started to miss the Malvern Hills and Worcester's city centre. Denise and I both longed to take a bath as showers only were available in the Guide house. I missed Marmite, which is odd as I'd never been a fan of it before. We both missed curry (which isn't even English, but it was freely available in England and unavailable in Tunisia) and we made a pact to one day buy a takeaway and eat it on the Malvern hills together. We never did, of course. Denise missed her family, which is obviously the most important thing to miss. But I had no family and I missed no one from England. I only made effort to keep in touch with Meena and the letting agency.

Here in Sousse, I now had a good situation - decent accommodation, a steady boyfriend, friends like Denise and Yetta, acquaintances like the Danish Reps who were great fun to be with. And so many other Reps from other European companies and friendly locals who worked in the hotels. I had free meals in posh hotels, an interesting culture, and the best weather possible. I could show my guide-card and walk into any nightclub for free and I could even take a friend in with me. So I either went in with Rouge or other Reps. But I didn't frequent the clubs too often. I always had to preserve energy for Repping.

It was my job to accompany our clients, on coaches, from the Sousse hotels and then all the way to Tunis airport. This would take approximately three hours, one way. The first hour would be spent going into the reception of around ten different hotels and checking our clients and their luggage, onto the coach. Then a two-hour journey to Tunis. At the airport I would see the departing clients and their luggage off, through passport control. Then I would meet the other Transfer Reps from the other resorts of Hammamet and Nabeul and we would usually chat a while, over a quick airport lunch.

Then at arrivals, we'd meet and greet the new clients. I'd cross them off of my manifest list and direct them to the Sousse coach. While the other Transfer-Reps found their own clients for their own resorts. Half of my coach journey back would be spent talking over the microphone. As we passed through the capital, I would point out places of interest, the tree-lined avenue of Habib Bourguiba, important buildings, and other streets and some history of the country. Then I would proceed onto a Panorama 'Welcome talk' which included general information on the weather, the culture, trips and excursions (which our company was selling at a profit) and where the clients could locate their Hotel Reps for the duration of their stay. It was essential that the new holiday-makers went along to their Welcome meetings - tomorrow, to get information to have the best holiday ever. (But really, the main reason was for the Hotel Reps to sell the trips and excursions.) Then the bulk of the journey was spent answering an abundance of questions which the excited new clients usually had.

All in all, the round trip took approximately seven hours if the flights were on time. And I would make this journey six days a week. But there were often delays and we Transfer Reps could be left waiting hours for a problematic flight load. A percentage of the clients would usually be in a foul mood after being delayed and we would be the direct receivers of their wrath. But we were to always smile and apologise profusely. Sometimes we would fall asleep in the airport café, while waiting for a delayed flight, and then someone (one of the many airport workers) would nudge us awake to tell us the flight was in. We'd quickly run to the toilets, splash water on our faces and redo our makeup. The joke was that we painted on our smiles. And that 'A good Rep was a pale Rep' because we never had time or energy to go to the beach and pick up a suntan. We were tired all the time and looked generally white and pasty. Another motto was 'Work hard, play hard' but most of us preserved our energy for the working hard part of that saying. The 'Work hard play hard' reps never lasted more than one season apparently. It was just too exhausting.

I, myself, was sent on excursions, for free. I had to know the tours well to appreciate what I was selling to the clients. The 'Desert Safari' excursion was an eight-hour coach journey (with holiday-makers.) Then a camel ride in the Sahara at sunset. An overnight stay in a basic hotel with evening meal and breakfast early next morning. (I saw a cockroach the size of a small mouse in my hotel room there but that's another story.) Then an eight-hour journey back to Sousse.

I'd gone to the overnight desert trip on my day off and Denise had been obliged to cover my airport-run next day on her day off. I would often forego my once-a-week days off for trips or the covering of the Hotel-Reps duties, while they were obliged to go on trips. But although I was generally exhausted, I was content with my situation. Much more content than I had been in recent years. If I was upset with Rouge or disappointed about something else, in my life, at least I had Denise or one of the Danish Reps to talk to, which was of some comfort at least.

I also went on an inland excursion to the 'Great Mosque of Kairouan,' which was a striking building both outside and in. And another trip to the 'Tunisian Night Out' in Baloum where fire-eating Fakir, belly-dancing displays and meals were included in the price, (although it was obviously all free for me.) They were nice trips but none of us Reps wanted to take them because it was just so tiring. But we had no choice. We were known to be in a sort-after and privileged position and there was a queue of thousands, back in the UK, ready and willing to take our glorious jobs from us if we wanted to quit. Those wannabes all thought that we spent our days on the beach and evenings in the night-clubs. But we rarely had any time or energy left for stuff like that.

In some ways we were privileged though. We lived, for free, in a tropical paradise and if we wanted to change destinations, we could request another location season on season. (Obviously the married Reps had to stay put.) Our pitiful wage would only count as pocket-money by English standards but locally we were seen as rich. Apparently, if a Tunisian married a Rep, he'd financially hit the jackpot.

We were highly respected by the hotel staff in general and this was another privilege. We could eat in any of our hotels for free i.e., any of the hotels which housed Panorama clients. And we would have the best table and service of a three-course meal with wine and coffee included, all for free. On the days we could coordinate it, Denise and I usually chose the most beautiful five-star hotels for our evening meals together. If we were in uniform, we were directed straightaway to our table. But sometimes we'd had time to change into our own clothes and in-time the waiters would recognise us anyway. But if they didn't recognise us, either Denise or I would simply say 'Ana Guida' meaning, I'm a guide, and we'd be seated immediately, even as a priority over our own clients! I was never treated so well as I was treated in the Tunisian hotels, we felt like VIPs, well actually, we were VIPs.

I heard so many stories of English women and girls getting used and abused by unscrupulous locals and I saw it with my own eyes, many times. A new girl or woman, traveling alone or in groups of females only, would be especially targeted. Those who were recently broken-hearted or in the process of bereavement were particularly vulnerable, especially if they were naive of different cultures, as most were. It was a sad thing to witness. Over time I saw several women in their sixties holding hands with young men who were young enough to be their grandsons. But young and pretty girls were not exempt from falling for the charms of the local guys. Basically, females of all ages past the age of sixteen, were seen as fair game. They would always be fed the same lines, that 'love doesn't have an age,' that it was all 'no problem.' Even if the woman was past the age of child-bearing and with a young man, it didn't matter as it was 'Love,' pure and simple.

The women seemed as though a spell of hopefulness or madness had been put onto them. Something to do with the sand and sea. It was all entrancing and the guys knew exactly how to take advantage of European-feminine weaknesses. It was a complete and utter abuse of trust. A crime as far as I'm concerned. Most English women seemed to have a default of automatically believing what was said to them. And that was our own fault (or the faults of our Fathers, Uncles and brothers, as far as the locals were concerned. English society hadn't protected their women and girls and so it was our lookout. If our mothers hadn't warned us and our fathers, uncles and brothers hadn't kept us on a tight leash, then as far as the locals were concerned, if we were over the age of sixteen then we were ripe for the picking.

English (and other European women's 'boyfriends') would hold their hands and look them directly in their eyes and promise to God that this was love. They might even go as far as marriage. They had nothing much to lose and everything to gain. They might receive presents, meals in nice hotels, sex, trips to England, leave to remain in the UK. There they could earn and send money back home to ultimately build a house for themselves and for their future real-wives who would bear them children. It was like watching a conveyor-belt of females coming and going. The dodgy guys were drawn to the tourist's zones, along the beach front, and they were apt at knowing all the right moves. They even schooled each other on what to say and how to play the game. They called it 'Business.' Some of the English women were so trusting and some of the Tunisian guys were so unethical. It was a perfect disaster zone in many cases, but not all. There were honest and genuine guys too. And occasionally, true love stories did take place. But this only served to lead others into a false sense of security. If you were in love, it was hard to know if it was true or false.

One time I told Rouge about an older English woman who was being taken advantage of and was about to make the mistake of marriage. And Rouge laughed, which upset me. There was nothing funny, as far as I was concerned, about vulnerable women's lives being ruined!

At least I wasn't in that position. Rouge never showed any interest in going to England and he didn't seem bothered about me being a Holiday-Rep either. He didn't seem to be searching for the jackpot. He didn't seem bothered about much at all.

I used to chat with a lovely female Tunisian Receptionist at one of our hotels. 'Why do English women give everything to boyfriend without marriage first?' she asked.

'Well, if we like him, we want to do it as much as he does and we want to show him by giving ourselves,' I replied.

'Then he will take from you, maybe once or a hundred times and then he will go to another,' she said.

'Well, I have Rouge and he's not like that,' I insisted.

'Il passe le temp c'est tout,' she said, in a kind but informative way. Then she repeated in English, 'He passes the time, that's all.'

Chapter 19

Professionals

I'd been in Tunisia for nearly six months, summer season had finished and the winter season had begun. My bank statement was finally forwarded to me from England. And that's when I discovered that my two 'professional tenants' hadn't paid their rent! They hadn't paid a thing since their initial deposit, of which the agency had taken their upfront letting and property management fees. But the agency had vetted them and they were 'professionals,' surely doctors or teachers at least. But they hadn't paid a penny. And the mortgage payments had come directly out of my redundancy money and now, next to nothing was left in my bank account! I was thrown into a state of long-distance panic and quandary.

I went directly to the office in the Guide house, where I lived, and called my friend Meena. She promised to do a bit of digging, about the agency, on my behalf. When I called her back a couple of days later, she'd discovered that the two 'professional tenants' weren't doctors or teachers. In fact, they both flipped burgers for a living, at McDonalds. Now I had nothing against this kind of honest work but it was surely a breach of the agents contract when they'd promised me 'professionals!'

I could achieve nothing by telephone and had no choice; I would have to return to London to seek a solicitor. I needed to sue the agent for breach of promised agreement and to send a 'notice to quit' to the tenants. Otherwise they might continue living in my flat where I was responsible for the mortgage payments. They were paying nothing and I discovered that my bank account was nearing empty. My Rep wage wasn't nearly enough to cover the monthly mortgage payments which had been collected these past months. I needed them out and new paying tenants in, as soon as humanly possible!

Luckily Yetta was sympathetic and made arrangements for me to have a week off of work and two seats (one there and one back) were saved for me on our company's chartered-flights, for free. My colleagues would cover my Tunis transfers which would be extremely hard for them on top of their other duties and I was incredibly grateful.

Meena was kind and helpful and convinced her parents to allow me to stay with them as I had nowhere else to go. I was to share her double bed - that was so good of her.

I flew to Gatwick then got myself across London to Meena's in Ilford, East London. I dropped my bag off there, then went directly to see the same solicitor in Forest Gate, who I'd used during the Andy saga. I was furious. The agency had lied to me and I wanted them sued. They needed to pay the months of rent which were missing from my account. Three quarters of my redundancy money had gone on me paying the mortgage while these freeloaders lived in my property for nothing, (the rest had gone on Zowie rent and living costs for my first two months in Tunisia.) Also, Meena had got the impression that these two so-called 'professional guys' were friends of the agency guy, who I'd dealt with in the first instance. Meena believed the agent had taken advantage of me being a single female. He knew that I had no one to help me and that's why I needed an agency in the first place. I'd told him that when I'd first spoken to him. I told him I had no one and that's why I needed the agency so much! Was I stupid, was it my fault for being so honest, was I too honest?

The solicitor made notes as I ranted and raved about the situation. Luckily, due to me reserving the second bedroom (where I stored my belongings) for myself, this had given me certain rights in law. And the solicitor was able to draw up the 'Notice to quit' with immediate effect (which would cost me £210.) I was lucky, because I'd kept my belongings in the second bedroom it counted (in law) as though I still lived there, which meant that almost no legal notice was required. But suing the agency was not going to be possible. The two tenants worked at McDonalds, therefore, flipping burgers was their 'profession,' therefore it could be said that they were 'professionals.' I thought 'professionals' meant Doctors and Lawyers or Teachers at least. But it's a quirk in the English language and a loophole in the law. The lettings agency knew exactly what they were doing and someone was making a lot of money out of this racketeering. The two guys had lived rent free at my expense and after they'd finished at my place, I guessed they would do the same thing somewhere else. The agency had taken a month's rent and deposit up front and kept it as their fee so the only one out of pocket was me. There may have been a third party involved, the 'professional' guys probably never worked at McDonalds' either. They just had the paperwork from there for the agent to cover himself. Box ticking. The agent therefore appeared to have done everything 'correctly' and the tenants not paying wasn't his fault! What a great scam! A scam at my expense and no doubt at the expense of many others before and after.

The 'Notice to quit' was served immediately but I had no time to hang about and I needed to know that the tenants would move out directly. So, I bravely went along to enter the flat. I was terrified. But it turned out that I had no need to fear as the non-paying tenants were long-gone by the looks of things. Their personal belongings had been removed and only some rubbish and mess had been left for me to clean up. I don't suppose I even needed to serve the notice to quit. So that was another £210 down the drain. In London, there are those who play by the rules while others are ducking and diving and living in another realm altogether. Well, I guess that's not just the case in London but all over.

I only spent two nights at Meena's and after that I stayed at the flat. I had so much to do. I threw out items which the two guys had left behind, got the locks changed - again, cleaned non-stop and contacted another letting agent. But this time I lied. I said that I would be popping back to the UK often and I gave Meena's contact details (with her agreement) as my UK contact. So at least it looked like I had backup. I explained that I had brothers and cousins in the area too but I said I didn't want to burden my family with rent collection unless there were issues. I'm not sure the agency believed I had brothers and cousins when I'd given an Asian girl's name as my contact. But I'd done my best and hopefully the agency was now convinced that I had some backup at least.

I briefly met the nice young couple as they moved into my flat and that must have been a good thing. They knew my face and I knew theirs. Then I left for the airport. On my return flight, I reflected on how, sadly, honestly wasn't always the best policy.

Chapter 20

Serious

I was back in Sousse where the winter season was in full swing. Back in a country where the locals followed a book of rules which us 'tourists,' as they called us, didn't understand. We played by a completely different set of our own western rules.

We didn't see much of the Tunisian girls and women, although many worked as Chamber Maids in the hotels. They tended to not speak English and generally kept a low profile. Most of the hotel receptionists were male with just a few females. On my rare conversations with the female receptionists, who I knew, I'd learned that their attitude towards men was completely different to mine, and the English women in general. They looked at men in a completely different way to the way we did. For them, it was all about respect and marriage and being supported and protected by men. While for us it was all about love, freedom, sex and equality. I disagreed with the Tunisian girls on just about everything at the time and I pitied them for their lack of freedom. But with hindsight I agree with them on a lot of things and envy their stability and security. From my life experience, girls need protecting, not only from males but especially from themselves. I may sound old-fashioned by Western standards (so please excuse me, it's probably due to my life experiences.) Anyway, I was no longer a girl. I was now a woman and I'd reached an age where I seemed beyond all of it now anyway.

Rouge loved to speak other languages and he especially liked to practise his Swedish with the Danish Reps who spoke several languages. I got jealous and angry one night when he kept forcing the language back into Swedish and the only words he said in English were that Swedish was his favourite language. Then I was thinking about this respect thing and the marriage thing. I was thinking about how the Tunisian girls saw life. Up until then I'd thought that they were oppressed while I had the 'freedom' to do as I wanted. No one was oppressing me or guiding or correcting any move I made and no one was loving me either. I was confused about it all.

Rouge had never shown any interest in coming to England or marrying me. He didn't seem to be after my Rep wages either. He didn't drink alcohol at all or smoke weed, so this all seemed excellent for considering him as a potential husband. He cared a lot about his own family and seemed family orientated, which was exactly what I was aiming for. I wanted someone who prioritised family because I thought that that would one day include me. But I was starting to realise that the whole 'Little house on the prairie' situation was likely an impossible dream. I was without structure, without my own family, without my own community, without direction or purpose. For long term relationships, on paper, I was now not such a great catch myself, especially in Arabic culture.

I was wondering if I was too damaged and incapable now anyway? There had been loads of warning signs over the past few years including the Christmas dinner that I'd been invited to with Ritchie's family. I just hadn't been able to cope with a 'normal family' even though it was what I longed for most of all. Or maybe because I longed for it too much and didn't have my own to match it. It was off-sided, bent, tilted and unbalanced, likely impossible now. And what was I really doing in Tunisia? Yes, I loved the atmosphere, the weather, the food, the Arabic language and the smiling faces of the holiday-makers. I loved that people knew my name and recognised my face and seemed pleased to see me. These were all good things for my present but what about my future. I wanted children and I wasn't getting any younger. I loved Rouge but did he love me?

Rouge ticked a lot of boxes. But he'd never introduced me to his family. I'd asked him, a few times, to clarify what our situation was and at least twice he'd said, 'We are friends,' and 'We are friends that's all,' which didn't seem like he was very serious about me at all. But we had, had a nice evening out on my twenty-eighth birthday at the end of September. (I hadn't had many good birthdays to look back on since adulthood and this was a nice one to remember.) Rouge had taken me out for dinner and given me a pair of bespoke, antique silver-earrings shaped into my name in Arabic. This seems very thoughtful, kind and romantic. It wasn't that I was desperate to marry him but I just wanted the reassurance that he was serious about us and not just 'passing the time' as one Tunisian girl had suggested. The birthday evening had reassured me somewhat, that he did have feelings for me at least.

Soon it was Christmas and Denise had managed to get some favourite food items sent over from her mum in England. We threw an impromptu party on Christmas day at the Guide House, with our Danish house mates. We also invited other Reps and their boyfriends, coach drivers and office staff. Lots of people came but Rouge didn't show up. I was again disappointed.

I knew that I was in love with Rouge and something had to be done about the pain of it. So, the next time I saw him, I had it out with him. And this is what he said, 'You are at the age where a woman wants children and so I can let you go and do that.'

'You mean without you?' I spoke.

'Yes, you can go find another one.' He replied.

'But what about us?' I retorted.

'We are friends, that's all,' he said.

I was upset, disappointed, and frustrated more than ever after that conversation. Rouge couldn't have made things clearer really. But as he still smiled and held my hand and we still talked and had fun together, it was hard to accept that a future for us was out of the question. Perhaps in time he'd love me more, if I was just patient?

Being with Rouge was a constant and confusing competition between my head and my heart. Of course, we still saw each-other after that but not so often as Rouge would sometimes let me down by not showing up. I kept trying to justify why he kept letting me down. And I'd make excuses for what he'd said about it being time for me to have children with somebody else. He didn't mean it like that, he meant it like this. But I guess I knew, deep-down, that Rouge was never serious about us. And I was starting to question my own motives about what I was really doing with my life here in Tunisia.

It was a February evening and Denise and I were sitting in the café opposite the Guide house. We were drinking coffee and chatting about the day we'd just had. Denise had had some troublesome clients in one of our hotels and her day wasn't even over yet. A client had had her bag stolen at the medina and now Denise would have to take the woman, and her husband, to the police station to make out a report. That was something we Reps all hated doing because the police were so difficult to communicate with. Not just because of the language barrier but also because of their attitude and general arrogance. Some of them seemed to have some kind of God complex, probably due to their positions of power. I'd had a delayed flight and an angry client complaining all the way to Tunis airport that day. This was nothing unusual. It was pretty much a 'run of the mill' day. That was until I went to the toilet for a pee.

When I sat back down to finish off my coffee, I suddenly had the worst pain in my abdominal area. Denise was a trained nurse in the UK and she could see that I wasn't joking. She went onto automatic pilot, telling me to wiggle my toes and take deep breaths. Perhaps it was trapped wind or something, she said. 'Sit up straight, lean back, perhaps it's cramp.' She spoke. Sitting up all day for seven hours to Tunis and back, every day, probably wasn't good for me. We both expected the pain to pass in a few minutes but it only intensified.

Denise then helped me up to my feet where I bent over double in excruciating pain. Like that she helped to nudge me across the road and back to my room in the guide house. She ran to the office and immediately called our doctor. She was so sorry to have to leave me to suffer alone as she had to accompany the bereft woman, and her husband, to the police station. This job always took hours. But our doctor would be along as soon as he could make it.

All of the Danish Reps were out at the 'Tunisian night out,' so I was left alone, rolling around in shocking pain and fear at what was happening to me! The doctor must have been terribly busy because he took a further two hours to show up. The door bell rang and he could see me, through the double glass doors, shuffling towards him. My long brown hair sticking to my sweaty face, I must have looked like the living dead!

The doctor instinctively knew it was serious. He lay me down and pressed around my abdomen region. Then he literally picked me up and carried me to his car where his wife and child waited for him. They spoke in Arabic to each other and then his kind wife tried to comfort me with words of broken English. But by now I was so delirious and in out of consciousness.

Within a few minutes, I was dropped off at the 'Clinic les Olivia' a private hospital. I was immediately wheeled in for Xray followed, in quick succession, to the scanning room. A male doctor and his male nurse discussed (in Arabic) what they could see. Then in broken French and English I discovered that I had kidney stones and one was passing, causing this excruciating pain.

I was then wheeled to a lovely private bedroom and given pain-relief and a saline drip. One male nurse stayed by my bedside all night! Every fifteen minutes I would ask to be taken to my en suite bathroom as I constantly had the sensation of needing to pee. He would help me up and then stand outside the door, calling through, in simple French, to make sure I was ok. A few hours later, the pain stopped and I slept. When I awoke, a different male-nurse was watching over me.

I was kept in the hospital for a further two days. The stone had passed, along with the pain, so I no longer needed pain relief or a constant nurse at my bedside. The hospital had delt with Reps before and they knew that the second I was let out I would be put straight back to work, so that's why they kept me in, for a rest. Denise came to visit me when she got the chance but although Rouge knew I'd been admitted, he never came.

From my hospital-bed telephone, I delt with the health-insurance people. Thank God I was fully covered by my company insurance. If this had happened when I was in the Zowie apartment, I would have had zero insurance and this wonderful service would have cost an absolute fortune. God knows how I would have paid for it. A loan perhaps, I've no idea. The only other option would have been the free hospital which was, by all accounts, an atrocious place to end up. But I guess either way I'd survive it.

I reflected on the ordeal which I'd just been through. I recognised that terrible pain as I'd suffered it before. When I'd lived with Mark at his place in Manor Park, several years ago. At that time, I kept going to the hospital and the obstetricians kept checking me over then sending me home! I'd rolled around in pain, back at Mark's squalid place but I never knew what was wrong. I'd always suspected that that severe pain had been partially responsible for the premature labour. At the very least, it had caused the doctors and nurses to ignore my cries when the real labour came. But I could never be sure of any of this.

Here in Tunisia, I'd been taken care of. The service had been excellent but then again it had been 'private.' After a good rest I was released out of the clinic. By the next day I was back doing the Transfers to Tunis. Everyone had been struggling with covering my duties while I'd been off and the company were not happy about it. 'A good Rep is a fit Rep' was another one of our mottos. There was no space for Reps who were not fit enough to do their jobs properly and rumour had it that I wouldn't be offered a contract for summer season.

I remembered that Yetta had once mentioned that a large company called Owners Abroad might be starting up in Tunisia. So, in a bit of a panic, I applied to their head office in England, for work with them, just in case. Nothing to lose. But apparently there had been no sign of them coming to this country as yet.

It was March and my latest London tenants were due to leave the flat in a few weeks' time. They'd paid their rent and everything was up to date. But they'd chosen to live somewhere else. So, I had to think about re-renting for a further six months.

I hadn't seen Rouge for a couple of weeks when he sent his cousin to come and get me. His cousin said that Rouge was in a night-club at the other end of the resort and I was to take a taxi right away, and meet him there. I wanted to go because I'm a mug in so many ways. But I decided against it. It was too much. He'd been standing me up, letting me down and I'd heard nothing from him for two weeks. And now he thought he could just click his fingers and I'd go running. I wanted to see him, I wanted to go but I knew I had to stop. I loved him but he didn't love me and I had no more time to waste here in this unrequited love situation.

The winter season was coming to an end and would coincide with my tenants (in London) moving out. Not a problem, the agency would put new tenants in, if that was what I wanted. But would they be good ones? I didn't want to risk bad ones. And if I did risk it, then what? Another season, another year? Other than improving my pigeon French and Arabic, I wasn't achieving much. I hadn't even been offered my summer season contract yet anyway. I had long come of age and I was exhausted from Repping, I needed a couple of weeks off. And I was thinking about quitting altogether.

Looking back, I'm not sure that Rouge ever thought seriously about me but I'll always remember his big smile on the night we first met. There was so much happiness and hope then. But as our relationship had gone on, it never really developed and I always got the impression, in the back of my mind, that when it came to marriage, he would choose a young Tunisian girl. That's why I was so surprised when I heard that he'd gone to Sweden to visit his Swedish girlfriend! Perhaps he'd planned on telling me this on the night he'd sent his cousin to me, a couple of days before he left. I bet she was beautiful. I bet she was stunning. I bet she kept him on his toes and didn't throw herself at him. I bet she had a family supporting her. Maybe he would marry her. But maybe I dodged a bullet there, who knows.

I felt such a fool. Should I stay in this foreign land or was now the time to return to my homeland? I knew that if I stayed, I could end up in a much worst situation than I'd done with Rouge. At least he'd only 'passed the time' with me. I'd seen much worse things happen to other English women. One Rep, from the resort of Hammamet, was married and escaped to England during the night, leaving her two young sons behind. In Tunisia, the children are the property of the man, so she couldn't legally take them with her. She wouldn't have got them through passport control without the documentation of her husband's permission for his children to leave the country. If she'd have attempted it, she would go straight to jail. I don't know how bad it would have to be for her to have left her boys behind. Pretty bad I should think. But then there were other women who seemed to be treated well, those who seemed happily married with children (like Yetta) so it was all very perplexing. As life is in general.

I'd made a decision; it was no use me staying. My job was insecure, my London flat was too. And Rouge didn't love me. I'd given him a year and all he could say was, 'We're friends.' And now I'd heard that he had a Swedish girl!

No, it was time for me to leave this foreign country, the land I loved and felt attached to, sometimes more than my own. 'In my dreams I'd been to Tunisia.' I would always have a place in my heart for that weird and wonderful land. I hated it there and loved it so much.

I'd managed to accumulate so much stuff in my year abroad. A handmade rug, an Arabic lantern and a bloody Alibaba laundry-basket! How ridiculous would it all look back in my concrete London flat and how would I would get it all back there anyway, I just didn't know. But luckily, we had special privileges on our charter-flights and it was all packed into the main-hold.

I had a window-seat and the in-flight background music was already playing as the aeroplane was taxiing, ready for take-off. But I zoned out completely.

'Oh, ooh, oh do we not sail on the ship of fools?'

'Oh, ooh, oh why is life so precious and so cruel?'

You know that feeling, when the aeroplane lines itself up, ready for take-off and then the pilot suddenly puts his foot down and you get thrown into the back of your seat, from the force. You fight against it to squash your face up tight against the window and watch the palm trees getting smaller You know, it's over, and you know you'll never live that time again. And you know you'll never-ever see his face again. He put a spell on me, that one, the red one.

I had to take a minicab from Gatwick airport because I couldn't even carry my belongings. London looked the same as ever. Grey and with a million faceless faces. So much hope and so much misery. And then onto the east-end which was even grimmer.

Would it or could it ever turn around for me? I'd been on the wrong track from years ago. What were the options now? Work, a new boyfriend, the flat. Or I could go off again. Somewhere new. Maybe that was an option.

Chapter 21

Lodger

I was doing some housework, one afternoon, when there was a knock on the door of my ground floor flat. There was a tall dark-haired man and a slightly shorter dark-haired woman, standing there. I didn't know them and they were saying that they'd come to 'see the room' I was renting out! I realised and told them that they'd obviously got the wrong address. But then I said, 'Actually I do have a spare room which I could rent out to you.' And then I invited the couple in. They were very pleasant, a brother and his sister. It turned out that it was the man who needed accommodation and his sister was just accompanying and supporting him in his endeavour to find somewhere to live.

Ryan had recently separated from his long-term girlfriend. They'd lived at the other end of Forest gate and they had a two-year-old daughter together. He was keen to find lodgings, close to his child, so that he could keep up their relationship. He had a look of desperation in his watery eyes and I sympathised with his rotten predicament.

I showed Ryan, and his sister, the spare single-room, which was still full of my own clutter at the time. Then I made the two of them a cup of tea and discussed the lodgings rate. Then I gave them my telephone number and suggested Ryan still find the original place that he'd intended to search for and decide between the two properties. I needed time to think about the idea too.

The following day, I received a telephone call from Ryan. He'd found and seen the original room in a house down the street from me. But he'd much preferred my flat and my situation in general. We reached the agreement that he would become my lodger. He would move into my second bedroom in a couple of days' time.

The day after that, I received a letter from Owner's Abroad, the UK based holiday company I'd applied to just before I'd left Tunisia. They were inviting me to come along for an interview the following week. I agreed to the interview although I was unsure that I would take the job if offered anyway. But I figured I had nothing much to lose by interviewing. I could decide or decline afterwards.

Ryan seemed like a decent kind of guy who'd fallen on hard times. When he turned up, with all his belongings, it was pouring with rain and he was soaking wet. He was bedraggled and seemed nervous and lost. It turned out, his long-term girlfriend no longer wanted him and she'd thrown him out and he'd been sleeping on his sister's settee in the interim, until he'd found me. Moneywise he was in trouble as the authorities were now involved and he was obliged to pay a large percentage of his reasonable wage (as a bank clerk) to child support. Would it be ok if his daughter stayed over at the flat with him on occasion, he'd asked. Well that was no problem for me but how would they manage in a single bed in the single room?

'You know what, you can have the double room if you prefer?' I spoke.

'Really but, but how much more rent would that cost me?' Ryan hesitated to ask.

'Nothing more,' I replied, 'I don't mind being in the smaller room and there's a possibility that I might be going off abroad for the summer season anyway, so it would make sense that you have the bigger room in that case. If I do go, all I ask is that you look after the flat, forward my post onto me and pay your rent regularly, directly into my account, oh you would be responsible for the utility bills of course,' I continued.

'Well yeah, that would be no problem at all, what about a deposit payment?' he questioned.

'No need for a deposit, just pay me a month's rent in advance, starting today and on the same day every month, oh also, if I need you out, for any reason, I'll give you one months' notice and you do the same for me, if you decide to leave,' I insisted.

Ryan had fallen on his feet. He would now pay the same rent for a single room while having the double. Also, there was a chance that I would leave him the run of the entire flat at the same cost as the single room. That's what you call a result. But, in my mind, it all depended on how we got along and I was undecided about going off again either way.

Ryan looked as though a huge weight had been lifted off of his back. We spent the rest of the day rearranging the two bedrooms and he settled into the big room. In the evening I split my dinner with him and we chatted. He was good company even though he was obviously suffering mentally, I suspected clinical depression. I was no stranger to that and we got along fine.

I had no romantic interest in Ryan; he was so fragile. And I didn't seem to be attracted to fragility in men, maybe because I was too much inclined that way myself and opposites attract. But I was happy to have him as a flat-mate and perhaps, in time, a good friend. A friend in need, a friend indeed.

Good news, Mandy had moved out from the upstairs flat and a pleasant African woman had moved in with her two young children. But I decided to keep my distance, I'd learned my lesson when I'd got too close to Mandy and I'd never make the same mistake with neighbours ever again. I would always be polite with 'Good mornings' et cetera but I would not have neighbours inside my home again and avoid going inside theirs, rightly or wrongly.

Over the next few days, I got along well with Ryan. He seemed to grow in confidence with every passing hour and I felt pleased to have helped this once stranger. The situation had helped me too. He was good company and with his rent I had options. If I were to stay and look for work, the rush to find it would be less pressing. Also, I felt sure that he was trustworthy enough to be left alone, which gave me the option of going Repping again. His small rent wouldn't cover the mortgage, of course, but the Repping wages were double with Owners Abroad to what they had been with Panorama. This turned out to be because most of their destinations were in Europe (more expensive for living costs) rather than North Africa. (But they were in the course of spreading worldwide as well) So, I felt confident about the option of more Repping too.

I decided to go along to the interview process, chances are I wouldn't even get through the first round anyway. Apparently, there were always thousands of applicants for very few positions. I knew it was a tough process and I'd only been lucky by being in the right place at the right time when I'd being taken on in Tunisia. Still, I had nothing much to lose by attempting with this new company. The interview was to take place in central London.

It was the first stage and interview time. We needed to be fit, funny, enthusiastic, a people person, fluent in at least one European language and good at sales. On top of that, we had to be able to either sing, dance or act!

I said I was fluent in French which was really stretching the truth and if they tested me, I would surely fall at the first hurdle. But luckily for me, the interviewer was only fluent in Spanish. When she asked me to speak French, on the spot, it didn't matter that I'd dropped in a couple of words in Arabic by mistake and that my French conjugation was atrocious. I could have gotten an award for speaking only in the present tense and waving my arms about for past and future! When asked about my thespian skills, I said I was 'a Singer' and like that, I blagged it though to the next round, along with only fifty percent of the other hopefuls.

The next round was a group interview. We were called through into a conference room, in batches of ten at a time. We sat around a large oval-shaped table, looking at each other intensely. Most of us, in my group, were female but there were a couple of young men with us too.

Two male leaders came in and starting talking about the job and how tough it would be. One asked if any of us had previously worked as Reps and only two of us put our hands up. The other girl was immediately told to stand up to tell the group about her experience in Majorca and I waited my turn as I knew I'd be next.

You might get the impression that I was now, suddenly, a very confident individual. But I think I'd just reached a point of not caring or I'd gone passed caring about what other people thought of me. Especially people who I didn't know in life which was - everyone. My analysis of this is that everyone reacts to trauma differently. One of my side effects of trauma, was confidence or moreover the appearance of confidence, especially in talking to people. But it wasn't confidence in the true sense of the word, it was more like a kind of performance. A protective wall of performing confidence. But it wasn't fakery, my bubbliness was now a part of me, ingrained in me. I think I'd learned that people are attracted to smiley people so when I felt down, I hid myself away. My misery had never attracted anyone other than psychotherapists and counsellors! Whereas smiling was attractive and important especially in customer-facing roles such as Holiday Representatives. Holidays are meant to be the happiest two weeks in people's year, so they don't want their representative being on old misery guts. So, for us Reps, it was always Show Time!

I stood up and introduced myself. Then I told the leaders and the group, that I'd just returned from two straight seasons in Tunisia. One male Leader interjected, 'Tunisia? You're brave!' He spoke. I smiled and continued by telling of the country's culture and how it was for me as a Transfer Rep there. Then I told the group about the desert safari and the other excursions I'd been on there.

'If I were to give you this scarf and ask you to sell it to the group, how would you go about it?' Said the other leader, as he removed his scarf from his neck, threw it towards me and I instinctively caught it in my right hand.

With the scarf still in my right hand, I walked to the front of the conference room and stood next to the two leaders. Then I began, 'This scarf comes in a variety of colours, it's a blend of nylon, wool and cotton and, (I forcefully threw the scarf on the table) it's one hundred percent, unbreakable!' I picked the scarf up and continued, 'It retails at £9.99 but, it's yours today for only £4.50!' I handed the scarf back to the owner with a wink and he took it with a hint of surprise.

By the end of the group interview session, I didn't really care if I'd got the job or not. I'd got the impression that another season would be full-on with this company and I really didn't know if I even had the energy for it.

Chapter 22

Canary Islands

A few days later, I received a letter, I'd been offered Children's Representative (Known as Kiddie Rep) for the summer season in the Canary Island of Lanzarote. I only accepted the job as I just didn't really know what else I should do with myself. And I suppose I felt that my personality was suited to this line of employment. I was a people person with good customer services skills. I basically just smiled a lot, I smiled in the face of adversity, which is an essential quality for Holiday Reps.

I was in for a rude awakening over summer season. The whole experience of working with Owners Abroad was completely different to what I'd learned as a Tunisian Rep. If I thought Tunisia had been tiring, I now really had to be full of fun, energy and resilience.

I flew to the island of Gran Canaria on a Wednesday with a connecting flight to the island of Lanzarote. The company wanted me immediately and didn't want to wait for the following day when there was a direct flight! A tall, beautiful blonde girl was waiting for me at

Lanzarote airport arrivals. She was holding a board up with my name on it, under the Owners Abroad logo. I walked towards her, pushing my heavy trolley. And she introduced herself as Candy. She claimed to be Deputy Head Rep, with 'Owners'

'You drive, don't you?' Candy spoke.

'Well yeah, I've passed my test anyway' I said.

'Av ya got ya driving license with ya?' She continued.

'Yes, I have' I replied.

'Ok let's get ya luggage into ya car' She went on.

We went out to a little green Panda and proceeded to haul my cases and bags into the boot and the back seats of the vehicle.

'Ok so ere's a map of the island, you'll be staying with the other Kiddie Rep, Cavey, you'll like er, she's a laugh. Anyway, ere's ya car keys. I'll see ya tomorrow at the weekly meeting.' And with that, Candy turned, jumped in another vehicle with someone else sitting in the passenger seat, and sped off!

'Oh my God' I said to myself, as I sat alone in the airport carpark, looking at the map. I was on the wrong side of the car, as far as I was concerned, the wheel was on the left with the gears next to my right hand. The opposite to what I'd learned in the UK. I was by no means an experienced driver and I felt I just didn't have the nerve to do it! I was overwhelmed.

I took a few deep breaths then I turned the key in the ignition and slowing drove towards the airport barrier which opened automatically. Then I pulled over to study the map again. My heart was pounding and hands were shaking. Then I started off again, but I drove the car in the completely wrong direction and before I knew it, I was nearing the top of a volcanic mountain. I didn't even know if it was extinct, active or dormant. I just knew I'd gone the wrong way and drove back downhill in a bit of a fluster.

I pulled over to try and calm down and to check the map again. I got my breath back, then slowly made my way to the motorway. I came off the motorway at the town of Costa Teguise and drove around in circles until I found the apartment where I was to stay.

I met my flat-mate, nicknamed Cavey (a Liverpudlian girl, a few years my junior) and we got along right away. She was not a driver and had been struggling to get to the hotel, where she worked as a Kiddie Rep, every day on foot. From now on she would jump in with me and we would work together. She told me the new Reps weren't usually given cars on their arrival but the Head Rep had told the team that I was a 'tough one' as I'd just spent two seasons in Tunisia. For some reason that meant I'd be able to cope with driving on the wrong side of the road in a completely unknown

Spanish Island! I suppose she was right, in some way, as I had just about coped. But I certainly didn't feel like a tough one, I was full of nerves but I had made it.

The next day, Cavey sat next to me, in the car, while giving directions. I drove to Puerto Del Carmen (the main resort) where our offices were located. I was introduced to the large team at our weekly team-meeting. Directly after lunch we all made our way to El Paso which was a restaurant/ entertainment club. It was a Thursday afternoon and we were to attend 'Cabaret practise.'

Charlie was another one of the Deputy Head Reps and he was not only the Compere of the show but he also seemed to be running it.

'Hi Jen, I'm Charlie, right then, do you sing, do you dance or do you act?' he demanded.

'Erm, erm, I don't know.' I replied.

'Well, you've got to do one of them so which one is it?' he continued.

'Erm, well I can sing a bit.' I spoke in an unconfident tone.

'Ok, so here's the list of backing tracks available, just pick any song that you know and we'll have you up on the stage in about ten minutes for a run-through. You'll be given a sheet with the words on, so don't worry if you don't really know them, I just wanna see if you can hold a tune or not.

'Shit!' I exclaimed, as Charlie left the table and I saw Cavey looking at me with an expression of excitement coupled with wild anticipation. And nervousness on my behalf.

'Can you sing? She questioned.

'Well, I guess I can hold a tune but I don't know if I can do it in public and up there' I pointed towards the huge stage.

Charlie was standing up on the stage when he called me over on the microphone.

'Jenny, have you chosen a song? Come on up and give us what you've got'

I'd chosen Top of the World by the Carpenters, only because I'd heard it so many times, I'd never sang it before. I gave my song choice to the Sound-Man and he gave me a song-sheet with all the words printed on it. Then I climbed the steps of the stage as Charlie passed me his microphone and I nervously looked around the establishment. The other Reps suddenly stopped chatting in amongst themselves and turned to stare at me. A spotlight flickered about and then landed on my shoulders. I felt like a nervous wreck. Then the first beats of the tune suddenly came on and I went on to automatic-pilot mode.

'Such a feeling's coming over me'

'There is wonder in most everything I see'

'Not a cloud in the sky, got the sun in my eyes'

'And I won't be surprised if it's a dream'

I was clinging onto the song-sheet and my hands were visibly shaking so much that the microphone was moving about. I felt sure that everyone was acutely aware of how terrified I was. It was hard to avoid feeling overwhelmed with self-consciousness and embarrassment. I took a deep breath as I continued grasping the microphone and staring at the song-sheet.

'Everything I want the world to be'

'Is now coming true especially for me'

'And the reason is clear, it's because you are here'

'You're the nearest thing to heaven that I've seen'

I knew the chorus off by heart, so now was the time that I needed to force myself to look up and attempt to put on some kind of performance. I took my eyes off the paper and looked out at the huge venue. It was empty other than a few tables with about twenty-two Reps who were just sitting and staring at me. And there were a couple of Bar-Staff members pottering about behind the bar but even they'd stopped what they were doing, to watch me up on the stage. I forced myself to fake some confidence as I moved my hips and tapped one foot in time to the beat.

'I'm on the top of the world lookin' down on creation'

'And the only explanation I can find'

'Is the love that I found ever since you've been around'

'Your love's put me at the top of the world'

Some of the Reps were swaying their heads in time with the music and I attempted a smile at them. The next verse was about to start and I took a deep breath ready to continue but then suddenly the music ceased to continue. And for a second or two there was an awkward silence.

Perplexed, I dropped the microphone to my right side and held it there as I looked over at the sound-man. He was shrugging his shoulders and pointing at Charlie who'd apparently giving him the signal to abruptly cut off the backing track. Blinded as a technician moved the spotlight into my face, I frowned at Charlie through the glare of the lighting. His silhouette came towards me, onto the stage and before my eyes could adjust to the detail of his features, he took the microphone from my hand.

'Ladies and gentlemen, you are now looking at our new resident Singer - Jenny!' Charlie announced. And with that the Reps and the Bar-staff started clapping as he covered the mike with his hand. 'You'll be singing that tonight at the Cabaret' He continued. Then during the week, we'll find another couple of songs, something a little more up to date.'

'Oh, erm, I'm not sure I can do that! I spoke. 'How

many clients are coming to tonight's show?

'Well, this venue takes up to two hundred and fifty covers but we've only got one hundred and ninety tickets sold, so far. But there's still time for more sales. It'll probably sell out, by tonight, it usually does. It's a sit-down meal with waiter service and wine and entertainments included in the price of the ticket. For £20 per person, it's a good deal and one of our bestselling excursions,' Charlie talked a lot. 'You can sing well so you're singing while the curtains are closed behind you and the scenery's being changed behind the curtains, for the next act. So, you might hear a bit of bagging and bumping but just ignore it and carry on.' I just stood there almost paralysed as my head spun with all this information. 'From next week you'll be doing two songs, one in the first half and one in the second.'

I felt sick with nerves at the thought of this evening's activities. As I came down the steps of the stage, Charlie spoke on the microphone again. 'We won't be needing you anymore, Debbie. Jenny's a better singer than you, so you're out and she's in.'

'Oh my God, the Reps are going to hate me,' I thought to myself. I imagined that this 'Debbie' would be so pissed off. I must have looked as though I had the weight of the world on my shoulders as I stood, aimlessly, at the foot of the stage. One of the Reps came over and introduced herself as Debbie. She wasn't bothered at all that she was no longer 'the Singer,' she actually seemed quite relieved.

That night I sang to a full house. I swear I couldn't even feel my legs, I was so overcome with fear. My legs were like jelly but the adrenalin rush and the words of congratulations afterwards, made it all worthwhile.

Chapter 23

End of season

I sang every Thursday, in the weekly cabaret, after that. The first few weeks were nerve-wracking but in time I got used to it and enjoyed singing in the thrill of the limelight. During my breaks from being either on stage or backstage I was to mingle with the audience where I was treated like a celebrity. Something I was not accustomed to but I took to it well and enjoyed all the attention.

The rest of my time was spent entertaining children, doing airport runs, attending office meetings, guiding pub-crawls, and taking notes on other organised excursions. Even my occasional days off were taken up with food shopping, washing my uniforms, and taxiing the other Reps.

My time in Lanzarote was very different to my time in Tunisia. From my experience with Owners, it was just bars and clubs and restaurants there. I was surrounded by English and Irishman and had very little opportunity to learn any Spanish. Relationship-wise, besides a couple of flings, nothing much was happening. It was Party Town and guys were just out for a good time. Maybe that's what the girls were looking for too. But not me, I wanted serious - so I only got hurt and felt used by this 'fun and free-love' dreamland, party island. Although I did have some fun, it wasn't really the ideal place for me. I felt there was nothing much to learn in Lanzarote and I missed my Tunisian lifestyle. In September I passed my twenty-ninth birthday and I was way passed coming of age. I mulled over what I was doing with my life.

Owners Abroad was a big company. Towards the end of the season our questionnaires were handed out to us at one of the last weekly meetings. We could chose/request our next destination and these destinations were now world-wide. When I was given the list of choices, I was surprised to see that Tunisia was now an option and I requested it as my next destination. I thought that I was in a strong position to get it. A, I had some knowledge of Arabic, French and Tunisian culture and, B, it had a certain reputation and a lot of Reps just didn't want to get it as their destination. It was a less popular choice.

It was October and we were coming to the last days of summer season. At our last official meeting we received our envelopes, with our following season's destinations. I was thrilled to discover I'd got Tunisia! How great it would be to see all of those faces again and to speak the languages I understood somewhat. The food, the sun, the white sand, (it was black volcanic sand in Lanzarote) and the Arabic music. And Rouge - of course I hoped to see him again. Yes, I'd heard he'd gone off to Sweden but that didn't mean he was still there. Perhaps he'd missed me, perhaps things would be different now.

I was so lost, living in between Lanzarote, Tunisia and England and nothing anchored me. The other Reps were excited to be going back to their hometowns in England. They would spend a couple of weeks with their families and old school-friends before going off to their next destinations. But I had no home-family, no true friends nor community. So, I clung onto the fakery and hope of Rouge, to cloud the truth of my reality.

I said goodbye to the Lanzarote team. We all promised to keep in touch, while knowing it wasn't going to happen. But there was always a chance that we'd bump into each other at our next destinations. Owners' sayings, 'Work hard Play hard,' (that was actually universal to all companies,) 'Party till you drop,' and 'Reps Never look back.' I returned to England with a two week break before the start of winter season in Tunisia.

Ryan had looked after my flat well enough. He'd paid the bills and everything seemed in order. Except that he was acting like he owned the place, my place. But I guessed that was kind of inevitable.

Ryan had gotten used to having the flat to himself

and now had to get used to me being back. But it wouldn't be bad, it was only for a couple of weeks and then I'd be gone again. But I found his behaviour irritating. And likewise, he was obviously irritated by me, I could feel it in the atmosphere.

Ryan seemed to have his young daughter over half the time at least. She would take bubble baths and get out covered in bubbles and then run around the flat, dropping water and suds into the carpets. He found it endearing and made no attempt to prevent it. This was a minor irritation which I would attempt to ignore. Ryan's irritation towards me was more of a problem. I was clearly getting in his way and on his nerves.

I had come across the Ashcroft 'coat of arms' which was a tiny little picture of a shield with a crest and a motto with 'Ashcroft' printed at the bottom. I didn't really know the significance of it but I'd decided to display it in my living room cabinet. I didn't have any real Ashcrofts in my life anymore and perhaps I was clinging onto something. I don't know but at the end of the day, it was my flat and my cabinet. Anyway, Ryan didn't like it being there and criticised me for it. He seemed to think that I was acting in a privileged/aristocratic kind of way by displaying my family coat of arms. In really, I was probably just clinging onto something that I'd lost a long time ago. But I guess he didn't know me well and was just assuming that I was acting like some kind of upper-class snob. I didn't like his misplaced and ill-informed assumption about my character but I had no reason to tell him my life-story either. I knew he didn't like the coat of arms being there so I begrudgingly removed it from the living room cabinet to a box in my single bedroom. I felt I could just about manage to suffer living with Ryan for another couple of weeks. At least I could trust him to pay his way. We were clearly irritating one another but it was for such a short amount of time that it wasn't worth making a fuss about.

After nearly two weeks of being back at my London flat, I received a letter from Owners Abroad. My destination had been changed and I was no longer going to Tunisia. I could spend winter season back in Lanzarote instead. I assumed that they had still not set themselves in Tunisia, properly yet. I was disappointed. I really didn't want to spend another season in Lanzarote. This restaurant/pub/club-lifestyle wasn't good for me. It attracted the wildest kind of party-animals. I was tired of it. But if I rejected this job offer, the alternative was grim. Life back in east London with no idea of what to do next.

After much soul searching, I turned down the company's offer of a second season in Lanzarote because I knew that nothing good could come from it. After I'd sent off the letter of refusal, I went straight to the department of social security and claimed out of work benefits. Due to my seasonal work coming to an end, I was apparently entitled to it. I didn't mention anything about Ryan staying with me as I'd already decided that our arrangement couldn't continue.

Ryan was devastated when I gave him his months' notice. I heard him crying in his bedroom one night, so much so that I had to knock on his door and tell him to come out for a chat. I made him a cup of tea and we sat and talked until the early hours. I hugged him and he cried in my arms. I did feel terribly sorry for him but our arrangement just wasn't working out. That night I promised him that I wouldn't chuck him out and he could stay until he'd found somewhere suitable. That seemed to help him a lot. It relieved the pressure.

In the end Ryan found another suitable place quite easily. But it was just a room in a shared house with several others. He'd been lucky to have the run of my place and he knew it. London is filled with sad and desperate people. Ryan was just one of them and I was just another.

A couple of weeks after Ryan had moved out, I was surprised to see two policemen on my doorstep. They asked me if I knew Ryan and I suddenly feared that he'd killed himself. Why did I assume that? Because I knew he'd been very unhappy, possibly suicidal, and it was the first thing which came to my mind as I invited the policemen in. I suddenly felt terribly guilty for making him leave.

The two police officers sat down in my living room and by this time I was already quivering in anticipation of what they were about to tell me.

'So, you confirm that you know Ryan?' Said the taller of the two men.

'Yes, I do know him, I did know him' I stuttered.

'In what capacity do you know him' The second officer interjected.

'Well, he lived here with me, he was my lodger.' I said, as I visibly braced myself for the shocking news.

'You seem very edgy,' said the taller one, 'are you ok?'

'Yes, can you just tell me what's happened to him?' I replied.

'Well, he has made an allegation against you. He says that you entered his room and took his credit card.' Said the second officer.

'What! What? I stared at the officers in disbelief, 'I didn't even know he had a credit card! So, if I took his credit card, what did I do with it?' I questioned.

'Well, that's what we've come to find out, have you made any transactions on Ryan's credit card?' The taller of the two asked.

'No, I haven't, oh my God, I can't believe he would say such a thing, is he lying or does he really believe what he's said about me, maybe he misplaced it and thought that I took it? I don't know' I said.

The two officers shook their heads at each other and then discussed how there was nothing to report on here. They couldn't tell me what they were thinking or any more details because of confidentiality but they reassured me that nothing more would come of it. I was to forget they'd even been to see me. With hindsight, I think they already knew that Ryan was the guilty one and they were just going through the motions by coming to check on his story. From my reaction, their suspicions of my innocence were confirmed and I heard nothing more on the subject.

It was obvious to me that Ryan had done something dodgy. Probably out of desperation, so in that case, in some ways, I don't blame him. I think he'd somehow spent a lot of money on the credit card, maybe with deliveries to my address and then tried to get the debt off his back by claiming I'd committed a crime against him. Perhaps he'd even ordered one or two feminine items in my size to make it look realistic. I would never know as the police were sworn to secrecy. I don't know how he could live with himself accusing me like that but it's amazing what people do, especially in a state of crisis, and nothing shocked me anymore.

Chapter 24

Fixing Roots

Without roots I felt like nothing, I felt like a nobody. My time abroad, being treated as a VIP and being surrounded by my teams and happy holiday makers, had only intensified my feelings of unwelcome solitude back in Forest Gate. I was like a ship floating around the ocean without an anchor. There was nowhere to dock, no place of anchorage. Sometimes I would float and there were times when I'd sail but I'd often be smashed into the rocks and almost drown in a ship-wreck. I couldn't settle, I felt useless and pointless. I would spend a third of my time in excited anticipation of new loves, a third was spent in a crisis of devastation and a third in depression. I'd had so much therapy but there was just too much going on in my head and they, the councillors and psychotherapists, didn't have a hope of untangling it. They only seemed to make me feel more hopeless.

Deep down I was still angry and devastated by my family's treatment and rejection of me, after my mother's death. I was still bereft. I was damaged in every emotional way and subsequent relationships had only added further trauma. Without the permanence of family and my place in the sequence of the hierarchical relationships, I saw little reason, purpose, or point in life. Unanchored I would continue to damage myself; it must have been a kind of self-harm. Friends would be good; they would be important but they would come and go. But family is the rock of life. Family is not an important thing, it is everything. But mine had been so fragile, so flimsy.

I realised my perceptions were badly fractured as sometimes I looked in the mirror and didn't even know who I was looking at. I sometimes looked at my belongings and wondered who they belonged to. I was having bad dreams and involuntary trauma responses and acting upon disorders that no one else could see. The narrative through which I saw the world was so badly fractured and yet I still had enough self-awareness to understand that I had to somehow find a way to knit it back together.

Perhaps I should try and repair my broken roots, to repair my relationships with those who had broken me. To face my demons in some way. But mum was long gone and I couldn't rebuild any kind of relationship with my estranged father or sister. They were the dragons who'd burnt me and I needed them to at least apologise profusely. They had to attempt to apologise at least. But how could they attempt to apologise without contact. I wasn't giving them a chance. I'd been too angry, too damaged, too disappointed and I still felt that way. But most of all, I was too afraid that they would hurt me again. The fear of emotional pain was my deterrent, which is odd seeing as I was repeatedly hurting myself in other ways, with other people. With Men.

Should I give my estranged family a chance? The jury was out. Some said I should never speak to them ever again. And that had been my plan so far but it hadn't felt great. Should I give them an opportunity to show me that they at least regretted their treatment, their neglect - was that the answer? Would it help me if I knew that, would it help them? Was that to be my potential cure? It's difficult when you're so angry and hurt because you look so vicious even if you try to cover your emotions, they can see it. They feel it. You look like a dog showing its teeth and no one wants to stroke a dog like that, even though it might need comforting.

I'd kept what I called 'a Christmas card relationship' with my sister Carol, so I had details of her new address. By letter, I made contact and asked if I could visit her in Worcester. She was now divorced from her first husband. She was remarried to a decent man and now lived in a house in an area called Brickfields (still on the same side of Worcester where we'd been raised.)

I knew that area well as I'd played in Brickfields Park as a child. It was so green. Part of England's green and pleasant land. I used to practice handsstands there. I'd found it somehow easier as the park was built on a hill - the hill which led up to the back side of Hollymount. My old home was there in Hollymount and all my family memories were inside, in that house, in the middle of that street.

My sister replied to my letter and seemed happy to receive me at her new home. She agreed that I could visit her whenever I wanted, which seemed a good start. The date was set and I was ready, ready to face my demons.

'Zipping up my boots, going back to my roots'

This old song had been in the charts in 1981 before I'd even left my hometown in 1982, yet I couldn't get it out of my head, as I made my way across London. Soon I was at the mainline and about to leave Paddington station. It was now 1993 and I'd been away from Worcester for the best part of eleven years already. I was no longer in my youth; I was a woman. But I felt that I'd failed to thrive due to my messed-up history and lack of support and guidance. The years were flying by but the shackles of the past were still on my feet, dragging me down and preventing me from dancing.

Maybe, to move forward, I needed to forgive those closest to me, those who had wronged me so. But how would I forgive without their apologies, without their repentance, without them begging for my forgiveness. And did I really want that, could I really stomach it. And how could they ever apologise or show me that they regretted their actions when I now had next to nothing to do with them and if I never spoke to them again. They'd always blamed me for their wrongdoing in the past, I didn't know if I was now able to cope with that possibility again.

These ideas had gone around in my head a thousand times and I was just too hurt and too angry to even consider putting myself back in my hometown. Over the years I'd convinced myself that I hated the place or that the city of Worcester meant nothing to me yet I knew, in my heart, that it meant everything. Denial had been my only way of survival up until now. But now, today, I was ready. Ready to face my damaged and broken roots.

As the train moved along the tracks, I relived the day that I'd travelled to London by myself at the young age of seventeen. I was now twenty-nine and I was doing that same journey again but now in reverse. I didn't recognise any of the stops along the route until I got closer to Worcester. Then it all came flooding back to me.

As the mighty Malvern hills crept up on me, I was overwhelmed with a combination of excitement and despair. The beauty of those magnificent old hills was spectacular and the strongholds of my trauma - automatic. Steady and solid, no matter what happened in my life, those hills never changed. Literally steady as a rock, like the anchors I lacked.

I walked out of Foregate Street station just as I'd walked in, all those years ago. And I suddenly thought that everyone would recognise me, that every other person would call out 'Hi ya Jen!' just like they had in the past when I'd know so many folks. But as I stood there in the city centre, waiting to get mobbed, the people walking by were unfamiliar and no one recognised me. I was a stranger in my hometown, surrounded by strangers.

I felt like Rip Van Winkle, in the old story of the guy that took a nap and fell into a deep sleep. He woke up twenty years later without realising he'd slept for so long. Over the twenty years of sleep, he'd grown a long and bushy beard and aged so much that no one recognised him and he knew no one in his hometown. He had no idea of what had happened and felt lost and confused.

People didn't know me now and I didn't know them either. I was the feminine version of Rip Van Winkle - without the beard. As I walked along the high street, in the direction of the bus stop, I stared at different faces. Some of them seemed to look familiar but I couldn't be sure if I was just imagining it and no one called out 'Hi ya!' as they used to all those years ago. It was a surreal experience. Almost an outer body sensation.

As I got onto the bus, I asked the driver about the price of the ticket to Brickfields. 'Hi ya Jen' he said, 'remember me?' He looked vaguely familiar but I just couldn't place him. 'I used to work at the swimming pool, I was a Life-Guard way back then, you was always there, ent seen ya for years, were's ya bin bab?' I'd forgotten about that broad accent and unusually incorrect colloquial speech. It hardly made any sense yet I understood it perfectly.

It was true, I had spent a lot of time at the swimming pool in my early teens. In my last two years in Worcester, I'd moved house so many times that I didn't know where I lived or who I was. I'd been shunted between father, sister, foster care and lodging addresses. (Until I'd finally given up at seventeen and taken a train to London.) But, the one constant had been the swimming pool. It's ridiculous and sad that the smell of the chlorine-bleach made me feel like I was home. The two other constants were the Cathedral and the hills.

This bus driver/ex Life-Guard would never know how much it meant to me that he'd remembered my face and my name. It meant so much and was all I needed to make me burst into floods of tears. But I held myself together and managed a little polite conversation about how I'd been mostly living in London. 'What's appened to ya accent, you'm posh now Jen.' The bus driver/ex lifeguard giggled.

I smiled and after paying, I took my seat at the back and remembered how, when we were at school, we used to always say 'Back seat agro' whenever we sat at the back of a coach or bus. Funny days. I missed my school friends; the boys always made me laugh in those days.

Thirty minutes later and I was at my sister's house. My nephew was now all grown up at twelve years old. So, although he knew I was his Auntie, he didn't really know who I was. My sister's second husband seemed nice enough and they all tried to make me feel welcome but the elephant was always in the room. A parade of elephants.

We didn't talk about it; it was too much. I didn't want to upset Carol and she didn't want to upset me. We were both afraid to even scratch the surface and the tip of the iceberg was already big enough. So, for a while it went on like that with certain subjects avoided, which was awkward and somewhat frustrating.

Then, out of the blue one day, Carol put her arms around me and said, 'I'm ever so sorry I let ya down Jen, I should av taken care of ya, but my first husband was such a bastard.' And the tears of regret ran down her cheeks.

This wasn't it; this wasn't the apology I'd wanted. Blaming others and making excuses. But it must be difficult to admit to such a crime, the neglect of a younger sibling and this apology was a step in the right direction. After all the years of wanting to hear a relative apologise, I'd rehearsed my response a thousand times. I had a million things I wanted to say. But I became completely tongue-tied and all I could say was 'it's ok' which it clearly wasn't. But from that moment on, perhaps it could be. With her apology, rightly or wrongly, perhaps I could start to forgive and then start to recover. It was like a huge container full of liquid and building pressure. Now there was a tiny hole in the container and over time the liquid would slowly release. I would let it release; I would make it release.

In some ways I knew that I would never completely recover but I decided I would try to be a forgiving person, for Carol's sake and for mine. Everyone is damaged, everyone makes mistakes, terrible life changing mistakes. I realised that the people who'd hurt me were messed up people and everyone's messed up. Everyone who hurts you is Damaged. We could never get those years back but I had to get rid of these shackles of anger and regret.

Now it was time to start practising with voluntary engagement of my traumas, rather than the involuntary trauma responses which often took me by surprise when I least expected. As I'd found it so difficult to relate to anyone, I decided right there and then, that I would write down everything that had happened to me, instead. I hoped that this voluntary engagement with my trust and abandonment issues, of past traumas, would prevent my involuntary responses and serve as some kind of therapy.

I can understand why people become religious now. Whether it's real or not. When all they can see around them is hopelessness, darkness, and misery - they look up out of desperation. I hope that they (and I) find peace and comfort there.

I walked uphill, across the park. I remembered the area so well. I was standing on the summit and I was looking down at the cathedral in the centre of the city. The Malvern hills stood there quietly in the distance, framing the scene. They were watching me watching them as the storm clouds gathered at their feet and all across the city. 'This is all I need,' I said to myself, 'I'm gonna get drenched and stand there all emotional, in the rain outside my old house, please - don't let it rain, not now.'

Then I walked downhill, just a little and my old primary school was there on the left. I could hear the children playing and yet there was no one there. I guess they were all in their classrooms and their laughter was in my imagination. Then I took a right turn and there stood my old house with all the memories of Mum, Dad, Carol, and our animals, Sandy the dog, Fred the cat and Flynn the rabbit. Their souls were all there, trapped inside. My soul was in there too.

I swear I could hear my dad practising his trumpet. Was that Fred the cat sitting on the living room window sill? Oh my, is that mum smiling and waving from my parent's bedroom window, and Carol is there too - what's she doing in my bedroom! 'Sandy you nutter, stop barking at Flynn!' I smiled. I turned again to stare at the hills as the clouds separated and dispersed and the sun broke through.

'When you look around yourself and all you can see is misery and disaster and you feel like you have no one to talk to, look up!' I looked up and took one last look at my house as the sun hit my old bedroom window, releasing its demons.

Whatever responsibility I could take for my own state, I had to grab with both hands now.

'Make it like a memory'

'Take away the sound and the sight'

'There'll never be another love'

'With the power of, you and I'

I walked the rest of the length of Hollymount with the sun on my face. It was time to leave Worcester again. I didn't live there anymore, it was over. But I felt I now had the freedom to return whenever I wanted. And maybe I would even return to live in my home-town again one day. It was no longer out of the question.

The shackles were now off my little ballet feet, so I

could dance.

Foot Note

Everyone needs meaning in their lives. I'd had such a negative outlook, I'd had trust issues, abandonment issues, I was an extreme people-pleaser, I wanted to feel accepted, to feel loved, to belong somewhere. But I never really felt any of these things until my son came along in 1996, followed four years later by my daughter in early 2000. Suddenly my heart was filled with love and purpose. Christmas, birthdays, Halloween, and Bonfire night all meant something for the first time since prior to 1980.

My children had no grandparents, no little house on the prairie situation. They were born and raised in London's east end in a multicultural, multiracial, and multireligious environment. A mixed-up society with no real sense of community. I did my best that's all I can say.

My daughter, as a psychology graduate, went on to become a Personal Trainer. Combining her love of fitness with sports psychology. And my son, as a Royal Ballet school graduate, traveled the world as a Principal dancer and teacher of ballet.

They say, 'it's better to give than to receive' and I always thought that, that meant presents and gifts. But now I realise that it means 'love.' I always thought I needed someone to love me, which is true, I did. But more than that, I needed to love, to give love, to give to someone who would receive it with grace.

Everyone is damaged in some way and no one is completely free from mental ill health. Writing my memoirs is a vocation which started off as therapy but went on to become a labour of love. My hope is that it might help someone to get through difficult times. To know there's always hope and a reason to continue.

Giving to everyone who suffers.

For you.

Printed in Great Britain
by Amazon